Puffin Books
Editor: Kaye Webb
STORM SURGE

The wind, which had been blowing at gale force all morning, was beginning to fling water over the sea wall, but no one on Flatsea Island was seriously alarmed. They were used to January gales and, besides, everyone said those walls were impregnable. So even when the creek stayed full at what should have been low tide, the little community went about its business as though it were any other Sunday.

And so no one was prepared when the water came surging through the walls that night, covering the bridge that joined Flatsea to the mainland and swamping the coastline too. Young Peter Brown was helplessly trapped in his family's pub, where the flood had burst open the doors and was rising steadily up the stairs, and was worrying desperately about what had happened to his brother Aaron, due back on the last train home after a night out in Oozedam, or to Martin, who lived on the mainland and had left with his girlfriend only a short time ago, or to his parents, who had driven into town to see their first grandchild, or to his grandparents alone in their cottage a little way inland.

David Rees tells his story of the flood and its aftermath with great power and clarity. You'll find yourself getting involved with every member of the close-knit Brown family as they face this crisis, whose shocking effect is, for more than one of them, a turning-point in their lives.

For older Puffin readers.

David Rees

Storm Surge

Illustrated by Trevor Stubley

Puffin Books

Puffin Books, Penguin Books Ltd,
Harmondsworth, Middlesex, England
Penguin Books, 625 Madison Avenue,
New York, New York 10022, U.S.A.
Penguin Books Australia Ltd, Ringwood,
Victoria, Australia
Penguin Books Canada Ltd, 2801 John Street,
Markham, Ontario, Canada L3R 1B4
Penguin Books (N.Z.) Ltd, 182–190 Wairau Road,
Auckland 10, New Zealand

First published by Lutterworth Press 1975
Published in Puffin Books 1978

Made and printed in Great Britain by
Richard Clay (The Chaucer Press) Ltd
Bungay, Suffolk
Set in Linotype Pilgrim

For
Terry and Harriet

Contents

A map of Oozedam and
Flatsea appears on page *18*

'The natural forces which bred the "great tides" came to be investigated, and investigation pointed to a phenomenon described as a *storm surge* ...

'It appeared that the "surge" was born of the drag of the wind on the surface of the sea, and had a fleeting dynamic life of its own, independent of the normal tide. The stronger the wind, the longer it blew and the farther it "fetched", the greater the increase of water it could pile up and set in motion ...

'If the peak of a surge occurred near low water, it was harmless; but should it occur near high water, at a period of spring tides, the combination might be deadly.'

Hilda Grieve
The Great Tide

Acknowledgements

I am indebted to *The Great Tide* by Hilda Grieve for some of the background information in this book. The definition of a 'storm surge' which appears on the preceding page is taken from her book and is reproduced by kind permission of the Essex County Council.

The quotation from *The Israeli Boat Song* by Lionel Morton which appears on page 80 is reproduced by kind permission of Essex Music International Limited.

D.B.R.

Part One
Flood

'They'll surely cancel the game? I don't know why you have to play on a Sunday anyway.' Charley Brown stopped cleaning the pipes and looked at Aaron, who was sitting on a stool on the other side of the counter, practising on his guitar.

'It's only because so many Saturday games have been postponed this January. I'll have to get there if I can. Look at that!' The wind which had been blowing at gale force all morning was beginning to fling patches of water over the sea wall. 'When's high tide?'

Charley looked at the pub clock. 'About now.'

'I'll go and see if the bridge is flooded.'

'Put your raincoat on.'

'Of course, Dad.' Why did people always point out the obvious, as if he had no common sense at all!

The gale took his breath away. He had to bend double to avoid being knocked over, and the force of it slewed him sideways across the road. The bridge was only a hundred yards off, but it took him nearly five minutes to reach it. The road was covered by a grey angry sea, the wind whipping a continuous curtain of spray off the surface and blowing it over the walls and far inland. Only the parapet was visible. He was alarmed; they were cut off from the mainland, for the moment at least. For how long? Perhaps he would not be able to get to his football match after all. He could not let the team down. Then a car emerged through the mist of spray and came slowly over the bridge. The water was not even a foot deep.

He waved, and followed the car back to the pub. His mother and his younger brother, Peter, opened the doors and ran inside. They had been into Oozedam to buy the Sunday papers and were full of excitement about the gale.

'There are trees down everywhere,' said his mother, 'and telephone wires, and people are pulling their boats right back to the edge of the road. With this wind and a spring tide tonight they're afraid of floods. Charley, I don't think we ought to go out this evening.' She folded her arms, always a sign that she was about to assert herself in an argument. She was a large imposing woman, formidable with customers who wanted another drink after closing time.

'Why ever not?' Charley, who was on his hands and knees behind the bar, sorting through packets of potato crisps, now stood up and faced his wife.

'I'm not leaving these kids on their own to drown in a flood!'

'Kids!' chorused Aaron and Peter.

'They're both strong swimmers, and Ron's hardly a kid. He'll be eighteen in a few weeks' time.'

'Neither am I,' said Peter, who was fifteen, and head and shoulders taller than his mother.

'Swimmers!' said their mother, scornfully. 'What do you think you're talking about, Charley Brown? I hope they won't have to do any swimming tonight!'

'In that case, Doris, what's the harm in us going out?'

'Because it's not safe, that's why not! If we're going to be flooded out we should be here ready to take the stock upstairs, instead of gallivanting half-way over the countryside!'

Charley planted his elbows firmly on the counter. Aaron

and Peter grinned at each other; Dad was going to make a stand. He did not often do so, but when he did, Mum had to surrender. Nothing would shift him. They thought it did their mother no harm to lose an argument occasionally.

'Now, look here, Doris.' He wagged his finger at her. 'You're just being hysterical. For one thing, there's been no flood warnings on the radio. Strong gales, they said, some rain and sleet. Cold. Nothing about floods.'

'If you go by what the weather people tell you, Charley Brown, you're a bigger fool than I thought.'

Aaron twanged out a tune to accompany the argument. He was the lead guitarist in a group he had started at school, and named after himself – 'Aaron's Rod'. They played at parties and dances in Oozedam, and had an occasional engagement at a disco.

'Secondly,' said Dad, counting off on his fingers, 'we're not gallivanting half-way over the countryside, we're only going into town, and we're going to see our first grandson. Gallivanting indeed! If we didn't go David would never forgive us.'

'That's not the point ...'

'Thirdly, Martin and Ann are coming in to look after the bar. They've done it before, and what's more, there won't hardly be any customers on a Sunday night with the weather like this.'

'I hope he puts a decent suit on instead of them jeans and beads he's always wearing.'

'Of course he will. And he knows this bar as well as you do.'

'As soon as it's closing time he'll be rushing off with her, and not bothering to wash up or lock the money away or anything.'

Martin was their second son, two years older than Aaron,

in digs during the week, attending art school in Ipswich. He had fallen out with his mother some months back, for instead of coming home at weekends he stayed in his girl-friend's flat in Oozedam. Charley told his wife it was none of their business, but Doris had never got used to the idea. Nevertheless, she was fond of Ann; Ann was an islander like the Browns and they had known her since she was a baby. She and Martin had been in the same class at school, and they had been going out together for years. Then last year her parents had been killed in a car crash; she had moved into a flat to be near her job, and Martin's visits home were confined to a few hours on Saturdays and Sundays, and Ann was always with him.

Charley pulled a pint of beer and held it up to the light. He invariably threw this first pint of the day down the sink – 'terrible waste,' Aaron always said, and his father would answer 'If you drank that one, my lad, you'd have the squitters by nightfall' – and then a second one was pulled, inspected, sniffed, and pronounced fit after he had drunk it.

'Well, Doris,' he said, as he tasted the second pint, 'you can do what you like. But I'm going to see my grandson. I've been looking forward to it ever since we heard. Kevin David Charles Brown. Grand names! Here's to him!'

'Can't we all drink to him?' Peter asked.

'No you cannot!' said Doris. 'The idea! You've done that already several times over. Ron, stop playing that blasted thing! It goes right through my head. And why don't you get your hair cut? How you can see on a games field in this wind and hair below your shoulders I don't know.'

'I wear a band.'

'I don't know what the world's coming to, I really don't. Martin decorating himself with beads and you with a hair-ribbon. I thought I'd brought four men into this world, not – not – I don't know what.'

She marched out, dignified but defeated, and slammed the kitchen door behind her. Charley and Peter laughed; Aaron played 'Land of Hope and Glory'.

'Do you think there will be a flood, Dad?' Peter asked.

'Do I heck! If there is my name's not Charley Brown. Last time the sea burst in was 1897; you ask your grandpa! And they didn't have sea walls like these. The bridge might be awash, nothing more. And that reminds me, what are you two doing tonight? Going out?'

'Youth club,' said Peter.

'I'm going to the flicks with John,' said Aaron, 'in Oozedam. "A Teenage Werewolf's Chick." Should be a laugh.'

'A teenage how much? Whatever next! Be back by half past ten, both of you. High water's eleven o'clock. The bridge may be impassable before then, and I don't want you stranded on the mainland.'

'Will do,' said Peter. 'We never wait till the last train. Susan has to be home by eleven.' But Aaron said nothing. He was planning to have a drink after the film, and that would mean catching the last train.

'Listen to it,' said Charley, as the wind lifted the dustbin lid off and sent it clanging across the yard. All the doors in the house were rattling, the windows squeaking discordantly. The mat by the front door lifted and dropped.

'Tide's turned,' said Peter. They all looked out. There was no more sea coming over, but large sheets of water lay on the land side, ready to work into the earth at the base of the walls and soften them. These defences were concrete on the sea side, but only at what were considered to be the weakest places. The wind outside screamed in the telephone wires, and roared in the leafless ash tree on the other side of

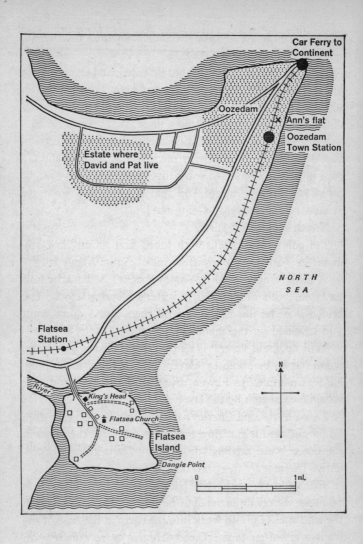

the road. Out across the island the marshes and fields were alive, moving ceaselessly as the wind rushed through the grass and flattened the reeds. A herd of cows huddled for shelter beside the wall of a barn. Angry clouds hurtled through the sky and a few flakes of snow dashed against the windows.

'You boys come and help me wash up,' said Doris reappearing. 'Haven't cleared away breakfast yet. Do you want a coffee, Charley?'

'May as well. It's an hour till opening time.'

During the afternoon Peter went out for a walk. He thought he would go and look at the sea, then return via his grandparents' cottage, which was a little way inland from the pub. Mum was still in a bad mood, and taking it out on him, as Aaron had gone to his soccer. A breathing space at Grandma's would be helpful.

The wind was less than it had been, but still strong enough to make walking difficult. The inn-sign, with its picture of Charles I's head, flapped backwards and forwards, creaking in protest. A huge branch of the ash tree had been torn off; it lay on the grass, a twisted, writhing shape, as if in pain. Peter turned off the road along a track through the marshes. He was glad he had put on his boots, for he had to splash through a large expanse of sea water before he could climb up the wall.

Flatsea Island was separated from the mainland by a narrow creek, crossed by the one bridge near The King's Head. Where Peter was standing it opened out into a large estuary that joined the open sea. On the other side was the port of Oozedam, a dark silhouette of houses, factory chimneys, cranes, and ships, against the grey sky. Lights of buildings and street-lamps made chains and necklaces in the dusk. When he and Aaron went to school, they crossed the bridge, and caught the train at Flatsea Station, just on the other side of the creek. It was the last stop the London trains made before Oozedam, and the line followed the edge of the land, inside the sea wall, for much of the way. The only movement now in the landscape, apart from the rushing clouds and the violent sea, was the lighted length of a train slowly leaving the town.

He turned and looked inland. Flatsea was well named. It appeared to be totally level, except for the little knoll in the centre where the parish church stood. Hedges and dykes criss-crossed the land, but there were few trees to break up the monotony, and they were all stunted or bent to strange angles by the winds that whipped in from the North Sea. The soil was poor, frequently waterlogged, and much of its grass salty from ancient drownings; until the walls were strengthened the sea had often swept in. Few crops were grown, but twelve families – thirty-seven people in all – lived on the island; a boat-builder, themselves, and a few small-holding farmers. Mum often complained that the milk tasted sour, and this was caused, she said, by the cows eating grass that grew on soil which had never lost its salt from the last submerging in 1897. But Doris was not a native islander. She had come from Oozedam, and had never quite convinced herself that she was going to spend the rest of her life on Flatsea. Peter and his father were proud of being islanders; the Browns had lived there for hundreds of years. He had once seen the names of his ancestors in the parish registers in the church; there was even a Peter Brown, 'son of Charles, fisherman, and Marianne, baptized ye fourth day of February, 1660'. He was pleased too that he took after the Browns in his looks; he, Aaron, David and their father were solidly built Anglo-Saxons, blue-eyed and blond in hair; Aaron's in particular was pale, almost white, the envy of all the girls. Only Martin was different, with friendly brown eyes and dark hair.

He was just about to climb down from the wall when he realized that something was very wrong. He had known it all the time he had been standing there, but only as a vague sense of unease; it was so obvious now that he could not understand why he had not noticed it at once. It was supposed to be low tide, but instead of the usual sight of glistening mud-banks, sloping down to a narrow shallow stream of water in the bottom, boats lying askew at ridiculous angles on the mud, the creek was more than half full. He looked at his watch. A quarter past four; yes, low water. It must be the force of the wind stopping the ebb, and he remembered, from the talk of old men once in the pub, that such a thing could happen. But never in his lifetime had it occurred. He wondered how this would affect the next high tide. It couldn't be much higher than it had been that morning; there wasn't that much water in the sea. Besides, everyone said the sea walls were impregnable. They had never been breached. Water only came over the top when a gale like this morning's blew, especially at this time of the year, January, and that was nothing to worry about. Still, he thought he should tell his father.

At the door of his grandparents' cottage he paused for a last look at the view. Though it was almost too late to see anything he could just make out the straight lines of things, the sea, the creek, the opposite shore. Everything in this landscape was horizontal, grey or black, except for the odd vertical post sticking up out of the marshes, or the spiders' web of Oozedam's cranes. But most of his vision was filled with a vast sky as clouds tore from the distant sea and billowed out above him. He loved it.

The cottage was a world quite different from The King's Head. It had a musty smell which he associated with churches, with very old people. It was full of ancient family relics, old china and old glass neatly stacked on open shelves; an old table he hardly ever saw properly as it was always covered with a thick red velvet cloth; armchairs from which the springs had long since gone; a dim sixty-watt light with no shade, flypaper dangling from it; pots of home-made jam and home-preserved fruit; souvenirs everywhere, inscribed jugs 'Time and tide wait for no man', 'A present from Aldeburgh', in a row on the harmonium. The most ancient relics he often thought were his grandparents themselves, Fred and Bessy Brown, both in their mid-eighties, slow and creaking with arthritis.

Grandpa was asleep in his armchair, but Peter's hand lifting the latch woke him. 'Bess! Come and see who's here!' he shouted, as if he had not set eyes on Peter for months. He saw him every evening in The King's Head.

'I can't come in,' came a thin, querulous voice from the kitchen. 'I'm baking. You see to it, Fred. Get rid of him, whoever it is.'

'She's going to Tilbury next week, boy,' Grandpa explained. 'To your great-aunt Sal. She always takes her own food with her. In case Sal tries to poison her off, I reckon. Daft, isn't it?'

'So you'll be on your own? Does Mum know?'

'I shall be right as rain. Always enjoy myself when the old girl goes off for a day or two. I'll be down in that there pub every night till closing time.' He laughed, which turned into a prolonged fit of coughing and wheezing; his face went purple, and he spat into the fire. 'Too much smoking when I were young as you are,' he whispered hoarsely. 'Don't you ever start that nonsense, boy.'

22

'Grandpa, there's something wrong with the tide. The creek's half full though it's low water.'

'Was it now? Hasn't done that for years. Means a very high tide tonight, top of the walls. Might even come over a bit. Nothing to worry about, with them walls. They'll keep her out. 'Twas different in '97, but you've heard me tell you about that time of day many a time. Now, talk about what's important. How's my first great-grandson?'

'I haven't seen him yet. He was only born yesterday, Grandpa.'

'They say he looks like Charley. Glad of that. Didn't want him looking like David's wife. Colchester girl. They don't make good-lookers in Colchester. Glad he's a boy, too.'

'Why?'

'Always make boys in the Brown family. Hasn't been a girl for a hundred and two years, Aunt Honor that was, and no good came of her.'

'Why, what did she do?'

'Went bad in London. Wicked place, London.'

Grandma came in. She was wearing an old hat, as she invariably did indoors. It was fastened to her hair with a huge hat-pin. Peter couldn't remember when he had seen her bare-headed. He wondered if she wore it in bed.

'Well, Fred! Why didn't you tell me who it was?'

'You didn't ask me, that's for why.'

'You old fool! Are you hungry, Peter?' She went into the kitchen, and returned with a plate of apple turnovers. 'My old aunt Alice's recipe. Going to take them up Sal's, show her what cooking is. She eats nothing but things out of tins.'

Peter tried one. It was delicious.

'You can take some home with you. Charley looks as if he could do with a feed-up. You going to church tonight?'

'No, I don't think so. Youth Club tonight.'

'You should go. Not often we have a service on the island. Only once a month. Not like the old days.'

'That Susan Allgood, she go to your club?' Grandpa asked. 'Seen you walk her home a time or two.'

Peter blushed. 'Nothing in that,' he muttered.

'My grand-dad married an Allgood. Elizabeth Allgood she was. Your Susan would be her great-great-great-niece. She would be that, yes. Nice old girl she was.'

'Fred, do leave off. You're making the lad embarrassed. What an old gossip you are! Always on about that time of day you are. By the by, you are taking me to church, aren't you?'

'Me? I don't know about that.'

'Fred!'

'I'll think about it.' He eased himself onto his feet and moved slowly to the door. 'Just going to make sure them chickens are shut up proper, Bessy. It's going to be a rough night, and we don't want them flying out to sea.'

'I'd best be on my way too,' said Peter.

'Take them turnovers. Wait a minute and I'll find you a bag. And that reminds me, I've got something for your ma.' She went upstairs, unsteady as Grandpa, pausing for breath. Peter pulled a book from the shelf. It was a cookery book, published in 1820. He was just reading a recipe for fruit cake which began 'Take twenty eggs' when Grandma returned, holding a patchwork quilt.

'I've just finished this,' she said, smoothing it out flat with long strokes of her hands. 'It's a cold winter, and it'll be colder yet. Someone down at home might be in need of it.'

'It's beautiful! A lovely thing! Can I have it? For my own?'

'Of course you can, boy.' Grandma looked foolishly

pleased. 'But it's nothing special. I've made dozens of them in my time.'

'It *is* special!'

'Tell your ma not to wash it, never. It'll spoil.'

Peter struggled home. The wind was rumbling under corrugated iron roofs, tearing at the ash tree, throwing cold sleet in his face. He clutched the quilt tightly to himself. It was not often that any of the grandsons returned home from Grandma's empty-handed.

'Can I get up now?'

'Yes, it's finished.' Martin threw down the paper on which he had been sketching. She came over to look.

'Not bad. I think that's the fifty-third drawing you've done of me.'

'You should be flattered.'

'I'll go and make tea.' Ann went into the kitchen. Martin picked up the *Sunday Times*, glanced at it and put it down.

'Listen to that wind!' The windows jumped in their frames and the door was impatient of its catch; even the flames of the paraffin heater flickered. The lampshade swung gently, casting shadows over the posters on the walls. Martin loved this room. Their books, his pictures stacked against the wall, their surfboards, the furniture, his paints, nothing else; nothing more needed. He looked out into the street. It was a road occupied mostly by immigrant families from the West Indies who worked in the port. Two dingy Victorian terraces, two floors each and an attic; Ann's flat was an attic, with a view of grey slate roofs, television aerials, other windows, the level horizon beyond. Down below was his car, an old banger twelve years old that sometimes worked.

'Martin! Come in here and look at the sea.'

'What's the matter with it?' He joined her in the kitchen. At the back they looked out onto a tattered, overgrown garden, at the end of which was the railway embankment. Beyond that was flat ground, mostly allotments, with several sheds, chicken coops, even a few pigsties. They had once been woken up in the night by a pig squealing, and until they realized what it was they clung to each other in terror, thinking that one of their neighbours was being murdered in cold blood. On the far side of the allotments was the inevitable sea wall.

'Can't see anything wrong with it.'

'Don't you think there's too much sea? It's just about low water now.'

'Can't see much at all; it will soon be dark. It looks rough, certainly. Lots of white.'

Martin returned to the newspaper, not very interested in the state of the tide. Ann brought in the tea.

'What are you reading?'

'An article on marriage.'

'Ah.' She sat on the arm of Martin's chair. 'Does the author approve?'

'Yes. Why, don't you?'

'Not again, Martin, please. Yes, but not yet. Aren't you cold?'

'No.' He wore old jeans and old T-shirts in all weathers, never a vest or a sweater, unless it was really Arctic. He put the paper down, yawned and stretched. 'I suppose we'd better get ready to go over to the pub soon.'

'I wish it was summer. Are we going to Newquay again?'

'Barman and waitress. I enjoyed it.'

'You enjoyed the surfing you mean. Prancing about in that wet suit. Do you know that cost us about half what you earned?'

'You were nicer than the surf. What did you mean, yes, but not yet?' He pulled her down from the arm of the chair onto his lap, and kissed her. 'I love you, Miss Betts. I want to marry you. I want you for ever.'

'There's no such thing. Don't pretend.'

'There is.'

'I love you, Mr Brown, ever or not.'

'We're good lovers. That's not pretence.'

Aaron was lying in the great square bath after the game, splashing about happily with the rest of the team. This was the best time, the hot water thawing the cold out of stiff muscles, inches of mud dissolving or peeling back from the skin. He could lie back and float in a sensuous trance, all thought evaporating out of his mind. It was bliss. Or mess about, ducking people, smacking their bottoms, singing lewd songs; or discuss the game with other men who like him were no longer the important different cogs of a team or pattern, but ghosts shrouded in steam. It amused him to think how his sensitive brother Martin cringed every time he described it. They had won, against a team who should have beaten them. Aaron, on the left wing, had not scored, but he was not displeased with his performance.

John Hewitt, hobbling on crutches, his right leg in plaster from groin to ankle, was waiting for him. He had broken two bones in a nasty fall a fortnight ago; it had been a rough game and John swore that the opposing centre half had deliberately kicked him.

'You shouldn't have come in this weather,' Aaron said. 'And standing on that leg all the time.'

'Only two stations from home,' John puffed and panted. 'I wanted to see you, Ron.'

'Strange without you this afternoon.'

'I need a break. It's a drag sitting indoors doing nothing all day.'

Aaron helped him. They caught a bus into town.

'We'll eat at Mount's Café, then the flicks, then a quick drink before the pubs shut. Don't let me leave this sports bag in the cinema.'

'Sounds fine,' John grunted.

'And perhaps we can find a couple of girls.'

'With my leg in this state? Not a chance.'

'Put you out of action?' Aaron laughed. 'Good thing too.'

The King's Head was an old pub. Peter's bedroom was called King Charles's room, and though the present house was not more than a hundred years old this did not stop him as a child from having nightmares about the king on stormy nights. When the wind sobbed and the sea thundered and the curtains fluttered it was all too easy to imagine Charles's headless ghost standing at the foot of his bed.

There was only one bar, and on a night such as this with the sound of waves almost on the doorstep and the wind in the chimney it was a cheerful sight; there was only a handful of customers, but they would probably stay till closing time. The light gleamed on the bottles and glasses behind the bar, and the flames of the fire danced in the glass on the pictures on the walls – copies of ancient maps of Flatsea and Oozedam – on Charley's precious collection of horse-brasses, and on the king's grave face framed above the mantelpiece.

Martin climbed on a chair and took this picture down. He looked unusually smart in flared blue trousers, a new flowered shirt, and instead of beads, an iron cross dangling from a chain round his neck. He replaced King Charles with a painting of his own, a landscape of Flatsea in summer: soft white clouds, a gentle sea, flowers in the marshes.

'Is it straight, Ann?'

'A bit to your left.'

Peter came into the bar. 'That's better,' he said, admiring the picture. 'Much more suitable. It's good, Martin.'

'It's a present for Mum.'

'She'll like that.' He looked at it for a moment. 'I must be off.'

'Don't be late back.'

'I won't. We'll give you a hand with the washing-up.'

As he opened the door, a tremendous gust of wind blew Grandpa into the pub. The old man leaned against the door to shut it.

'What a night! Gale's worse than ever. You're not going into town, lad, surely? You'll never get back.'

'I'll be all right. Aren't you supposed to be in church?'

'I said I'd take her. Didn't say I'd go in. Gave her the slip at the church door, had a natter with Alf Brookfield, then came down here. Pint of bitter, Ann.'

'You're an old rogue, Grandpa. Good night.'

'Good night, boy. And make sure you're back well before high water or you and that Allgood girl will be spending a breezy night on Flatsea Station. 'Tain't a night for that sort of caper.'

Peter went.

'Think he's all right, Martin?'

'Why not?'

'Tide didn't flow properly on the ebb. It might come over the walls about half ten.' He noticed Martin's alarmed face, and added, 'Not to worry. It won't come in here. Only do that if them walls crumble, and that won't happen.'

'Are you sure?'

'Course I'm sure. Haven't lived all my life here without learning something about wind and water. 'Tis nothing to worry about. What you do on a night like this is make sure the animals are locked up fast, case the wind blows a door in, bring the boats this side of the wall, and people already done that. Talking about it outside the church. Mum and Dad get off all right?'

'Yes. Mum didn't want to go this morning, Peter said, and nagged about it all afternoon, but the old man wasn't going to miss the first sight of his grandson. Then when Peter told him that the tide was still several feet higher than it should be at low water he thought he should stay. So Mum changed her mind and said she wanted to go!'

'Rum, people are, when they fall out.'

'You can say that again. Particularly those two. I'm glad I wasn't here.'

The door opened. Bill Allgood and two other men came in. The curious state of the ebb tide was the main topic of conversation. Nobody was quite sure what it signified, and they were afraid of the conclusions their thoughts led to, conclusions that seemed so unlikely that they dismissed them. No one wanted to be the first to be accused of panic.

'Think I was doing the right thing, Fred, letting young Susan out?'

'She'll be all right,' said Grandpa. 'She's with our Peter. Suppose the worst did happen, just suppose there was a breach in that wall, they might be better off staying out the night in Oozedam. Your sister-in-law would put them up wouldn't she?'

'Maybe you're right. Joan would, certainly.'

But they all remained uneasy. Although the talk turned to other things, they did not listen to each other as much as they normally did. When the wind struck the windows with a gust that really shook them, or swept the smoke down the chimney into the room, they stopped and listened in silence, then rose half-heartedly, wondering if they ought to leave, but knowing there was nothing they could do if they did. More islanders came in and reported that the sea was already coming over the wall at Dangie Point, the far end of the island, more than two hours before high water. But it was expected there. It was the most exposed part of the island, open to the full force of sea and gale. Nobody lived there. In any case the wall was firm, and it was only the wind blowing the sea over the tops; nothing serious. Then a large party of people came in from Oozedam, town people in three cars out for a night's entertainment. They had noticed nothing unusual on their drive over, apart from tree branches on the road. They brought in a different atmosphere, suits and smart dresses, different accents; Martin and Ann were kept busy serving vodka and lime, gin and tonic. No, they had heard no flood warnings in Oozedam; nor was there anything on the radio. They found the locals' concern rather amusing. Grandpa and his friends ordered more pints and crowded round the fire, sucking on their pipes.

At half past nine Grandpa stood up to go.

'What time will Charley and Doris be back, Martin?'

'About half ten, I think they said. Though I should think it might be earlier, as Dad was worried.'

'Good. That's before high tide. Well, I'd better go and face the music, I suppose.' He reached for his walking-stick.

Martin laughed. 'Music is right. Grandma will be playing hymns on the harmonium as it's Sunday night. Look after yourself.'

'I will, don't you worry. 'Night, Martin. 'Night, Ann. Bill, are you coming? You can see me back. My legs aren't as good as they were for a storm like this.'

'He just wants safety in numbers,' Martin said, 'for when he sees old Bessy. She'll throw the saucepans at him.'

Bill grinned. 'Come on then, you old boozer, let's be having you. 'Night, all.'

All the locals left before closing time. 'Unheard of,' Martin said, but they obviously wanted to make sure their houses were secure, and reassure their wives. The Oozedam crowd drifted away soon after ten; the last to go were two young men who had been trying all evening to chat up Ann.

'I hope your parents won't be long,' she said, as Martin collected up the ash-trays and dirty glasses. 'I don't want to be marooned here for the night.'

'They'll be here soon. They'd phone if anything was wrong.'

He went to the window. The wind was blowing sleet against the glass; it melted in long streaks.

'I hate the roar of that sea,' said Ann. 'I can hear it above the wind. It sounds as if it's longing to drown us.'

'Here they are,' he said with a sigh of relief. The door opened. It was Peter and Susan.

Peter went to a Youth Club in Oozedam every Sunday night. He enjoyed playing table-tennis or snooker with his mates, or sitting in a group absorbing the talk, though he contributed little himself to the conversation. Sometimes there were dances, and he liked these too, more for the music than the dancing. He stood at the back, tapping his feet and listening, hardly ever asking a girl to dance. Susan was the only complication. Because they were the only two islanders who attended, and therefore came in on the same train, and left together, people assumed that Susan was his girl. He didn't mind their thinking this, for it gave him a kind of status in the group, but it was not true. Susan didn't seem interested in him in that way at all, and he could not decide whether or not he thought anything more of her than someone who just happened to be with him often. He always walked her home, sometimes holding hands, but that was all. 'How do you know when to kiss a girl for the first time?' he had once asked Aaron, who was changing into his trendiest clothes, obviously getting ready for a date. His brother had looked at him rather witheringly, and replied 'You play that by ear,' as if it was a new number for his guitar. It was not an answer that helped much.

The only way to find out whether he was really interested in her or not, he often thought, would be to ask her out, to somewhere other than the Youth Club. But he would be humiliated if she refused, and he might be bored with her anyway. He was thinking about this on the train home that evening, and he found himself, much to his surprise, asking her. It was almost as if the words had formulated themselves out loud without any action on his part.

'Yes, I would,' she answered.

'Where to? There's the disco where Ron plays.'

She hesitated. 'If you like.'

'You don't want to, then?'

'Well ... I don't really like dancing much. I didn't think, Peter, that you did.'

He thought a moment. 'I'll ask Ron,' he said.

'Why do you always have to ask him everything?'

He blushed, feeling dreadfully snubbed. His heart was beating louder than the storm outside.

'Look at the sea!' she cried. Changing the subject, he thought; she doesn't want to. I won't ask her again. But he turned his head and looked out of the window. The darkness outside and the reflected light of the railway carriage made it difficult to see much, but it was obvious that water was tipping over the wall, long tongues of it running down. Here the defences were solid concrete on both sides to protect the railway; and now there was a continuous stream down the inside, like water flowing over a dam. What he had thought was heavy rain slapping the window was spray slung by the sea. Between the wall and the railway line he could see reflections of the train blurred by the wind: more water. Nearer to Flatsea both wall and track rose very slightly, and it was some relief to find the sea still firmly on its own side. But the wind rocked the train violently on this more exposed section, and the driver slowed it down to a crawl.

'The bridge will be covered,' she said.

'Then we'll have to take off our shoes and paddle.'

He returned to his own thoughts. Did he really ask Aaron everything? Perhaps, now David and Martin had left home, he did rely on him too much. Not that he had ever been close to David; the age gap was too large. He was such a different person, anyway. David was the conformist; he had worked at school, and though he disappointed Mum by failing his 'A' levels, he had a steady job in a solicitor's office in Oozedam. He was married at twenty-one, and was buying his own house, and now he had a son of his own. He went to work every day in a dark suit, a collar and tie. Peter could not bear such a life. He was closer to Martin, who was thoughtful, generous, someone you could trust and look up to. He wished he was clever in the creative way Martin was. He missed his brother badly since he had gone to college. There was something about Martin that attracted people, honesty perhaps; you walked down a street in Oozedam with him, and so many people stopped him, 'Hi ya, Martin! When are you coming to see us?'

Spray again hit the window and Susan looked up, but Peter was thinking about Aaron. Ron was quite different. He was arrogant and secretive. He was the most intelligent, but

34

the laziest. He didn't care what people thought, teachers, any adults. He just lived for sport, and playing his guitar. And girls. Ron was the best-looking; no girl ever refused to go out with him. In every classroom Peter worked in there were messages carved on the desks about him, bleeding hearts and 'I love Aaron', 'Aaron Brown, superstar'. But Ron had never had a proper girlfriend; two or three dates and that was that. Peter thought Martin had a better life with Ann.

He was the bonehead of the family, the only one of the four who was not bright enough to do any 'O' level courses. He preferred working with his hands; when he left school he was going to find work on the island, with Geoff Fox, the boat-builder. He was determined on two things; he would never leave Flatsea, and one day he would become the land-lord of the pub. And he would get married, to someone like Susan, only it would not be her, of course.

The train pulled into Flatsea and jolted him from his thoughts.

'Come on, dreamboat,' said Susan. 'We're here.'

Half an hour in the hospital restored Doris to a very good temper. Baby Kevin was the most beautiful baby in the ward. It was quite obvious: his skin was so white and clean, not that horrid wrinkly red babies usually were; there he was, fast asleep in his little cot, and she longed to pick him up and cuddle him, only the nurse would not allow it. Pat was well too, no problems there; and Kevin did look so like a Brown! She was a bit disappointed he did not more re-semble her side of the family, though it was a comfort he did not take after Pat who was, after all, not that attractive, even if she was David's wife.

'Doesn't he look just like Ron? Charley!' She poked him in the ribs. 'I said doesn't he look just like Ron when he was born?'

'No.'

'Oh he does, Charley! Look at the little darling!'

'He takes more after Peter.'

'I think he's the image of his father,' said Pat.

Afterwards they drove to David's house. It was on a new estate a few miles to the west of the town. A typical modern house, Charley thought, far too tiny for a couple starting a family. More convenient perhaps than their living quarters at the pub, and less draughty, the sort of thing he would fancy when he retired, but definitely not when you hadn't been married long and had kids. Doris, convinced that David wasn't feeding himself properly, set to in the kitchen. She had been rather put out when he refused her invitation to stay at The King's Head while Pat was in hospital, and, certain as she was that Pat was not a good cook at the best of times, she started work on several of her son's favourite dishes. While she cooked, David and his father drank beer in the living-room. Charley found talking to this middle-class son of his a bit difficult. Peter he loved most, the exact copy of himself at that age. A day out fishing with Peter down at Dangie Point on a calm summer's day was his idea of perfect pleasure.

The meal took a long time, then there was washing-up, and Charley became increasingly anxious. High water might produce a flood worse than this morning's, and he did not want to be cut off on the mainland. He had promised Martin not to be late, and there was Peter out at the club, and heaven only knew where Ron might be. But Doris was not to be hurried. Now she had decided to come out she was going to make the most of it. She found several shirts of

David's that needed buttons, and socks with holes in the toes and heels; these had to be seen to before she would consider moving.

'He can't go to work, Charley, looking like a scarecrow!'

David sensed his father's worry and said, 'You can always stay the night here.'

'Mmm.'

Then a violent gust of wind sent something crashing down in the garden. Charley pulled the curtains and looked out.

'A piece of the fence,' he said. 'Useless modern materials, they won't stand up to anything.' He thought for a moment. 'I think I'll ring the police,' he announced.

'The police!' cried Doris. 'Whatever do you want the police for?'

'Do you mind if I use the phone, David?'

The sergeant on duty was certainly aware of the danger. There had been a lot of water inside the sea walls in many parts of Oozedam but they had not been breached anywhere. The tide was much bigger than predicted; it might even come up several feet more, for it was not yet high water. There had been reports of flooding in Lincolnshire and round the Wash, but he couldn't say how serious it was. They were warning people who lived in low-lying areas of the town to take valuables upstairs, and advising those who slept in basements to move out, just in case. Flatsea? He thought the bridge might soon become impassable, but there should not be much water over the walls. It was unlikely. Nevertheless, sir, it would be a reasonable precaution not to leave anything important downstairs.

'Doris, we're going. The police say the bridge will soon be covered. And it will be worse in the morning.'

'Well, in that case I suppose –'

'I'm going *now*. It's half past ten. With or without you, I don't care.'

He went out to the car. Doris followed, grumbling, with a half-darned sock.

'I'll take it with me,' she said. 'And post it to you.'

'Sorry, David, to leave like this, but Peter and Ron ...'

'Good night, Dad. Bye-bye, Mum.' They kissed. 'Safe journey.'

The car went off at great speed, tyres squealing, Doris protesting at Charley's recklessness.

'We had to wade,' Peter explained. He had pulled his jeans above his knees, and was carrying his shoes. Susan was wringing out her wet socks in the sink behind the bar. 'If you don't go immediately, you'll be here for the night.'

Ann glanced anxiously at Martin. 'We haven't cleared up yet,' he said. 'And we ought to wait for Dad.' He could not make up his mind what was the right thing to do.

'We'll wash up the glasses, put the lights out. It won't take long.' Martin said nothing. 'Look, I'm quite capable of tidying up this place.'

'Dad wouldn't like it. What do you think, Ann?'

'Not for me to decide, love.'

'Martin, I'm quite capable as I said. There won't be any burglars tonight unless they want a very cold swim.'

'Suppose Mum and Dad can't get back?'

'Listen, if you want to go, go now. If they are stranded, I don't mind sleeping on my own. Ron may be here soon, anyway.'

'What about Susan?'

'I'll take her home as soon as we've finished. Yes, and I'll make sure I lock up before I do. For goodness' sake, Martin, you'll only just get the car through now!'

'Well ... if you're sure ...'

'I'm quite sure. Even if Ron doesn't come in, I can manage.'

'O.K. then, landlord. As you say.'

Peter and Susan listened to the sound of the old car fading in the distance as it reached the bridge, then there was only the wind screaming and the pounding of huge waves, the smack of water as it came over the wall and hit the ground, the slap of the spray as it drenched roofs and windows. They washed up in silence, then went into the kitchen to dry their clothes.

'Do you want cocoa?' Peter asked.

'Please.' He poured milk into a saucepan. 'Peter, about going to the disco. I would like –'

'Forget it. I'm sorry I asked.'

'Peter, I didn't mean –'

'I said forget it.' He glared at her.

'Will you take me home?' she asked in a small voice.

'We'll drink this cocoa first.' He switched on the television. It was a programme about the Queen's visit to East Anglia the previous week, very boring he thought, but Susan, who was a sucker for royalty, quickly became absorbed. He didn't remind her that she had just asked him to take her home. She didn't have to be in till eleven, even though her parents would probably be hoping she would come home earlier, considering the weather and the tide. Cocoa in the pub kitchen was part of the usual Sunday ritual anyway, and she could damned well wait till he was ready. He was having no more nonsense from her.

His thoughts were interrupted by a strange noise coming from the floorboards. At first he thought it was a mouse scratching, then it became more continuous, a hiss like escaping gas. He went to the stove, but all the taps were turned off. He looked again at the floor, and watched in horror as water came bubbling through the cracks between the boards, at first in long lines, but they were rapidly spreading into a lake that would soon cover the floor.

'Susan! Look!'

She shrieked with fright, then ran to the window and threw back the curtains. The clouds had lifted and there was a full moon. There was no land any longer. The sea, black and silver in the moonlight, stretched from the kitchen window to the horizon. It was swirling past at speed, rising every minute, not in great waves and torrents, but in an almost orderly fashion, like a bath filling. The walls had held, here at least, but they were not high enough.

'Peter! We can't get out! I shan't get home! What'll we do?'

Do? What on earth should they do first? They must not panic. He banged his hands against his head; no thoughts would come.

'Take the money out of the till and get it upstairs. I'll try and get hold of Dad.'

He went into the hall and dialled David's number, but before his brother answered, Susan was back. The water was up to their ankles, black and freezing cold.

'What now?'

The important thoughts came to him. 'There's candles in the larder. And matches. And take the brandy from the bar. And any rugs or cushions you can find. Get them all upstairs. David?'

'Candles?'

'The water will fuse the electricity. David? The sea's in the house; it's almost up to my knees. Where? In the pub, you fool. Where's Dad?'

'They've gone.'

The phone went dead. The water must be in the wires somewhere. What now? What now? Martin. He dialled Martin's number, hoping against hope that it was David's phone that had failed, not his. There were three separate flats in Martin's house, one phone they all shared on the landing. Answer it, Martin! He must be home by now. Susan raced downstairs and floundered past him. 'I've left my bag and coat in the kitchen,' she said.

'Martin, the water's in the pub. I'm up to my knees ... police? No, I didn't think. You'll ring them? I'm getting upstairs –'

There was a tremendous crash as the three doors of the pub burst open simultaneously, a deafening wrenching noise of splintering wood, and a great wall of water surged towards him. The lights all flickered, and went out.

'Martin!' He was shouting, terrified. 'Save me! Save me! We're drowning!'

Aaron and John thoroughly enjoyed the film. It was, as Aaron had said, 'a good laugh'. The audience were mostly teenagers, who kept up a running commentary on the film's absurdity, accompanied by jeers, cat-calls and whistles, so that even in the genuinely frightening bits it wasn't possible to feel alarmed. Aaron was one of the ring-leaders in the rude remarks shouted at the screen.

Afterwards they went into The Waterman's Arms, which shut half an hour later than other pubs in Oozedam, as it catered for workers coming off the evening shift on the continental car ferries. There were not many customers; a few dockers and couples from the cinema.

Aaron looked round. 'Those two girls there. They were in the queue for the film.'

John looked at them. 'Slags.'

'They don't look so bad.'

'Come and work this machine.'

They drank and smoked, and played table football.

'They're looking at us.'

'Ron, why don't you get yourself a real girlfriend?'

Aaron concentrated on a difficult shot. 'To tell you the truth, I haven't met one I could be bothered with. I mean one to be properly interested in. I prefer the company of my mates. You in particular.'

'Compliments! But you often go out with a girl.'

'Yes. I like dancing, taking them home.'

'You're just sex-mad.'

'What's wrong with that?'

'Nothing, but I want more from a girl.'

'So do I. In theory.'

'Let's have another drink.'

Aaron looked at his watch. 'Quick one, or we'll miss the train.'

'And you were talking about picking girls up just now.'

'I thought they might fancy a free ride to Flatsea.'

'You're an idiot.'

It was not till they were outside that they had their first notion of anything unusual happening. A police car passed slowly down the street, broadcasting a warning that there was a serious risk of flooding within the next hour. Policemen on foot and a number of volunteer helpers were knocking on doors, advising people to move upstairs. Even this far from the quay they could hear the deluging sound of water, hammering and battering at the walls. John limped slowly, so Aaron put his arm round him to hurry him along. The wind was still very strong and bitterly cold, driving handfuls of snow-flakes horizontally before it, but the cloud was beginning to thin and the moon showed fleetingly between dark scudding shapes.

The train was in at the station, the last one for the night. There were very few passengers. They walked the length of it so that Aaron could discover if there were any unattached girls who needed their company. John grumbled a good deal, and eventually they climbed into an empty compartment. He lay his plastered leg along the seat, and his head against the window; Aaron sprawled on the seat opposite. The train did not move. After a while they began to wonder why, and Aaron stuck his head out. There was an argument going on between the driver and the station-master. The driver was saying there was so much water over the line ahead that it wasn't safe to continue. The station-master said he'd heard nothing official or indeed unofficial about it, and if the train wasn't out of his station in ten seconds there'd be hell to pay.

'Get this bloody old crate moving!' Aaron shouted, and ducked his head inside before he could be spotted.

The train did start moving at once, which made them both laugh, and Aaron made V-signs at the station-master as they passed. Then he lay flat on the seat, lit a cigarette, and listened to the wind and sea.

About three-quarters of a mile out of Oozedam the train seemed to collide violently with something. Their carriage tilted half over, then fell back into place on the rails. Aaron was thrown off his seat onto the floor, hurting his back, and burning his hand on the cigarette. He scrambled to his feet, dazed, and looked at John, who was sitting up, complaining of the pain in his leg. Aaron opened the window. All he could see was a mass of swirling water and debris rushing past, already level with the bottom of the door. He could hear people in other carriages shouting for help. His feet felt wet, and looking down he saw water oozing in between the bottom and sides of the door. He slammed the window shut.

'My God! I think the wall's burst!'

The water rose rapidly to window-level. Then a large lump of stone smashed the glass in. Both boys were hit by pieces of flying glass; Aaron had a cut on his cheek, John on his mouth. Water poured in, filthy and icy cold.

'Quick! Get on the luggage-rack!'

Aaron pulled John to his feet. John clung to the edge of the rack, heaving himself up, Aaron lifting his plaster-of-Paris leg as gently as he could. The water was above Aaron's knees when he pulled himself up onto the opposite rack. The lights grew dim, then went out. The water rose steadily beneath them.

'What are we going to do, John? How can it come in so quickly?'

'The land rises a bit on the other side of the lines, so the water can't spread out.'

'My God. And I've never had a chance to love anybody.'

He stretched his arm down. His hand went into the water up to his wrist; he held it there a minute to see if the level rose. It soon came up to his cuff.

'John, we're moving out of here.'

'How?'

'I'm going to open the window and swim out. Then, when I'm outside I'm going to pull you through.'

'You can't.'

'It's the only way. Get undressed.'

Aaron began to take his own clothes off. This was not easy as the roof of the carriage was only an inch above his head, and the buttons on his shirt kept catching in the net of the luggage rack. His sports bag was just by his face, and one by one, he carefully put his clothes in it and zipped it up tight. Then he slowly lowered himself into the water. It was so cold the shock of it made him feel faint, and he struggled for breath.

'Bloody hell! It will freeze me solid!'

He gasped, then at last plucking up courage, dived down and fumbled for where he thought he would find the window catch. He failed, came up for air, choking and cursing, then dived again. This time he found it and pushed down with all his might. It opened. He swam through and came up for air on the outside. He was dimly aware of other people further up the train doing the same thing. He could just make out the line of the top inch or two of the wall above the water beside him. He swam to it and heaved himself up. Further along a whole section of the wall seemed to have given way, and where it should have been a surging torrent of water was pouring through inland. There was no sign of the front carriage of the train; it must have been knocked sideways by the force of the broken concrete and was now totally submerged. He swam back, and carefully lifted out his sports bag and pushed it onto the train roof.

'John. Are you all right? Are you undressed?'

'As much as I can manage.'

'Can you lower yourself into the water?'

'Yes.'

'Keep one hand on the window-frame. Are you all right?'

'It's cold!'

'Come on. Put your head out. That's right. No. Don't hold on to the window-frame. Hold my hand. I'm going to swim away from the carriage and pull you.' They both sank,

45

and came up, spluttering. 'That won't do. Turn round and try and come out backwards. That's right. Now grip the edge of the roof and heave.'

John did as he was told, but the broken leg was the problem. 'I'm stuck. I can't move my right leg.'

'I'll climb on the roof and lie flat and haul you up.'

Aaron did so; the biting wind on his wet skin was even colder than the sea. He pulled John's arms with both his, but John was still stuck. He felt himself slipping head first over the edge, and in righting himself he accidentally kicked his sports bag off the roof. He cursed as he watched it spin away on the water. He turned back to John, and thought the water had stopped rising, though the violent movement of it backwards and forwards between the train and the wall as each succeeding wave through the breach pushed it towards them or sucked it back made it very difficult to be sure. It broke over John's head, then fell away leaving half his body visible, then swept over him again.

'Once more, John.' Aaron heaved with all his strength, but his hands were beginning to grow numb, and though John shifted slightly, Aaron could feel him slipping slowly out of his fingers. John fell back with a cry, and disappeared under the water. Aaron waited for him to emerge, five seconds, ten. No sign. He jumped back in the water, could feel him frenziedly struggling, could feel the bubbles of air coming from his mouth. He put his arms round John's armpits, pulled and pulled again, but he could not move him. The plaster-of-Paris leg was stuck in such a way that it was preventing the rest of his body from surfacing. Aaron came up, swallowing great gulps of air, John hanging onto his leg; and shaking his hair back from his eyes and mouth, he shouted 'Help! Help me! My friend's drowning!' A man came running along the roof towards him and jumped in.

John's grip on his leg was weaker. He kicked himself free with his other leg, for he could not help John while he was held like that. 'His leg's broken,' Aaron shouted. 'It's the plaster-of-Paris. It's stuck in the window somehow.' They managed to free him at last, and pull him onto the roof. The plaster was cracked in several places and beginning to go soggy. The leg stuck out at the wrong angle below the knee. But it was too late. He was unconscious.

They placed him as gently as they could along the line of the roof. Aaron lay on top of him, giving him the kiss of life. Nothing happened. He tried again. Again and again and again. The man crouched, watching.

'Let me try,' he said. Aaron moved over. After about ten minutes the man said, 'It's no good. He's drowned. There's no heart-beat at all.'

'No!' Aaron cried, and pushing the man away, he tried again himself. He went on and on, refusing to give up, but it was no use. John was dead.

He pulled John round so that he lay across the roof, then turned him over so that he lay on his front. There was less chance now of his being washed away.

Aaron sat shivering, cold to his very bones. The wind soon dried him, but left him even colder. He was wearing only his underpants, a smart new pair they had been, purple with fancy decorations in gold and silver. He had thought they looked sexy. He had never been so cold in his life, but it was nothing compared with the chill that had entered his mind and heart. Someone came towards him along the roof and put a jacket round his shoulders, but he hardly noticed.

As Grandpa opened his front gate he could hear the strains of the harmonium and Bess's reedy voice singing one of her favourite hymns. 'Looking this way, yes, looking this way, Dear ones in glory, looking this way.' It might be one of the tunes she liked best, Grandpa thought, but she never got the words right. 'Oh dear Lordy me,' he said aloud. He timed his entry so that he could throw open the front door and shout a stentorian 'Yes ! !' afer the second 'Looking this way.'

'Be quiet, Fred,' said Grandma, who had nearly jumped out of her skin in fright, and was now playing a sequence of discords. She was wearing her best hat. 'There, you've made it go all wrong.' She played a loud 'Amen' in F major and closed the lid with a bang. 'Now then,' she said, turning to him, 'where do you think you've been?'

'You know quite well where I've been. I've been there nearly every night for the last sixty-nine years. I don't know what you ask for.'

'One of these days, Fred Brown, I'm going to sue you for divorce.'

Grandpa roared with laughter, or tried to; it ended in a terrible burst of coughing, his eyes nearly falling out of his head. 'I shall defend it, my love,' he wheezed. 'My defence shall be that I love you more than ever. Fifty-one years we've been married, and I love you more now than the day I married you.'

'You've never loved anyone but yourself. Certainly not me. I sometimes think I'd have been better off if I'd never set eyes on you. I'm going to bed, and you can sleep down here.' She picked up their battery radio.

'Why, what do you think I'm going to do at my age?' She shut the door behind her, unpinning her hat as she went. 'Silly old cow,' he muttered.

He went out to the kitchen and made a pot of tea, then filled two hot water bottles.

'Here you are, my dearest,' he said. She was sitting up in

bed reading the Bible, and took the hot water bottles and the cup of tea from him in silence. Hymns came from the radio. He undressed and got in beside her.

' "When ye therefore shall see the abomination of desolation, spoken of by Daniel the prophet, stand in the holy place, (whoso readeth let him understand:) then let them which be in Judaea flee into the mountains: let him which is on the housetop not come down to take any thing out of his house." Matthew, Chapter Twenty-four, verses fifteen to seventeen. Them's good words, Fred, worth remembering. Listen to this: "But pray ye that your flight be not in winter, neither on the sabbath day: for then shall be great tribulation, such as was not since the beginning of the world to this time, no, nor ever shall be." '

'Leave off, Bessy, do.'

She clapped the Bible shut, turned out the bedside light, and with great heavings and shakings settled down for the night. She had not been long asleep when something woke her. Something was wrong. The air in the bedroom was unusually cold, and she could hear a tap dripping. Several taps dripping. The wind was still howling round the house, but the gurgle of water seemed to be inside. Also the moonlight was much brighter than it should be. 'Be quiet, Fred,' she whispered, as he snored like a furnace, and turned over, muttering something about the walls giving way. She looked out of the window. Everything was white, as if there had been a tremendous blizzard; but it couldn't be snow, not in that short time. Frost perhaps. She could hear cows roaring, in distress she thought. And wasn't that faint cry a human cry, the word 'Help!'?

She prodded Grandpa awake. 'Fred,' she whispered, 'get up. There's been a great frost or something. Someone's in trouble; I can hear them.'

'What are you whispering for, woman? Go back to sleep, and stop dreaming. I do wish you'd learn not to eat cheese of an evening.'

'Get up, get up! Someone's calling for help! There! There it is again.'

Grandpa too heard it. He got out of bed, grumbling and muttering, scratching his bottom. He switched on the bedside light, but nothing happened. 'Bulb's gone.'

'Funny. I only replaced it yesterday.'

He went to the window. 'Bessy. O my Lord. Just look out there! That's never a frost! You're getting to be mope-eyed as a bat. That's the sea! It *has* come over the walls, then. Oh what shall us do?'

'The sea!'

'All that whiteness is moonlight on the water. Why, there's ... there's ...' – he rubbed his eyes, disbelievingly – 'hardly ... not a single blade of grass! That's a tree sticking up! And it's up to the house. Look! It's all round the house! It's half-way up the walls!'

He turned to her and in the moonlight saw the fear in her eyes. Then he shuffled out onto the landing, Grandma following. The electricity was not working there either. But what they could hear made them stand still in dismay. Grandma had thought it was a tap dripping, but it was the sea in the downstairs rooms, breaking gently on a step half-way up the stairs, clinking saucepans and jugs and cups and vases in a dance on its surface.

'Is it rising?' she asked. He started down the stairs. 'Be careful, Fred. Don't fall in! Oh do be careful!'

'This step's wet, and the next one. And the one after that. Tide's turned, it's going down. Ow! I put my foot in it, Bessy. It's perishing!'

'The abomination of desolation.'

'What?'

'Spoken of by Daniel the prophet. Pray ye that your flight be not in winter, neither on the sabbath day. It is winter. It is the sabbath.'

'Stop gibbering, girl, and tell me what to do.'

'I don't know what to do.'

She sounded lost and helpless. He dragged himself back up the stairs, and went into the spare room at the front. From there he could see some of the other houses on the island, all drowned to the first storey. There was candlelight flickering behind some of the windows, and heads looking out. Again there came the cry of 'Help!' but it was fainter, and as he listened he heard a distant splash. Someone falling from a tree or a roof? There were no more shouts. He shivered.

Not far off stood The King's Head. Like the other buildings it was half-submerged. A dead horse floated in the water. He remembered his chickens, but with a lurch in his heart. They would all be drowned. He strained his eyes in the direction of the pub, hoping to see a candle in the nearest window, Peter's bedroom, but though he stared and stared he couldn't be sure. Like Bessy's eyes, his were growing dim with age.

After Charley and Doris had driven about a mile back into Oozedam, past the pre-war semi-detached houses to where the Victorian terraces started, they found a 'Road Closed' sign blocking their way. Charley paused for a moment, then drove round it. A few yards further on they met the water. It was just a pool here, wind ruffling its surface. He drove through it, as he could see the road emerging dry on the other side, only a few yards on. But round the next bend he could go no further. Here it stretched as far as they could see, a torrent rushing towards them. People were running ahead of it, trying to escape. The rows of houses seemed to shrink the further into the water they were; in the distance only the bedroom windows were visible. Charley reversed the car, turned it, and hurried back the way they had come, looking for a by-road that would take them through the lanes round the back of town.

At first neither of them spoke. It was exactly what Doris had feared that morning and Charley had ridiculed, and what he had been so anxious about at David's and she had ignored. They were afraid to speak to each other. The sleet swept down the windscreen; the wipers mechanically swished it aside. Doris sniffed and searched for a handkerchief.

'They'll be all right, Doris, you'll see.' Silence. 'We don't know if there's any flooding at all at home.'

'If it's covered half Canewdon Road the island will be well under.'

'Not necessarily.' He didn't sound convinced.

'It's Ron.'

'Ron? He's probably safest of the three.'

'I bet he's on the last train home. It's probably trapped half-way along the line. Charley, I –'

'Doris, if the sea had already come in the train wouldn't leave. And if it hadn't come in then he's probably arrived home without any bother. He's probably in bed by now.'

'In bed! He's drowned, I know he's drowned. Oh, Charley, I can feel –'

'Stop it! You're being a fool! If he got stuck in town he'd probably go to Ann's. He's done that before. You know he's missed the last train a few times, particularly when he's been taking a girl out.'

'Yes, the little tom-cat. But he wasn't going out with a girl. I thought you said he was going to the cinema with John.'

'Well, you know what boys of that age are, meet some girls they know at the cinema ... they wouldn't tell us, would they? I bet he's safe and sound at this minute, on a sofa in a front room somewhere with a girl, while her mother's in the kitchen trying to work out how to get rid of him ...'

'Do you think so?'

'Absolutely certain.' He knew it wasn't true. He knew that Aaron was the most likely to be in danger. He had gone out in old jeans and an old jacket; if he'd had a date he would have come home to change after the match.

They drove past David's, down a series of country lanes, then turned left onto another main road which took them back to the outskirts of Oozedam on the south-west side of the town. There was no flooding here, and Doris seemed a little more cheerful.

'Charley, what about Pat?'

'Don't be ridiculous. Her ward was on the fourth floor.'

'I don't remember the stairs.'

'We went up in the lift.'

They sped through a maze of back-streets, all dry, and onto the road to Flatsea and the south.

'And Peter, and Martin, and Mum and Dad?'

'Well, the sea may have come in. I'm not saying, mind, it has. But it may have done. It may even be in the house. But it couldn't in a million years be so high it would cover the house –'

'Cover the house! I –'

'– or even reach the top of the stairs. If they've got any

sense, and they have got sense, Doris, they'll be high and dry in the bedrooms. Unless they've done something very stupid, and Peter and Martin aren't stupid.'

'But suppose one of them went down to the cellar?'

'There was no call for anyone to do that. Bar was properly stocked, beer was on, and unless they've had about forty people in drinking barley wine all evening, which they won't, they'll not have run short of anything. I saw to it all this afternoon when you were watching telly.'

'Getting your tea you mean. Yes, I suppose you're right.'

The sleet had stopped. They could see the moon behind the clouds. The road ran parallel with the railway, on almost the same level. They could see massive waves out at sea, which from time to time hit the top of the wall with tremendous force, almost like an explosion; huge columns of spray were tossed into the air and dropped back or were hurled over the railway line and the road, hitting the car with a strength sufficient to push it onto the wrong side of the white line.

Charley braked sharply. The road and the railway had vanished. He drove on, but the water rose rapidly to the bonnet. He stopped, revved the engine madly to prevent it cutting out, and reversed back onto the dry part of the road. Water was pouring across in front of them with the speed of a mill-race, taking with it what looked like quantities of seaweed and torn-up tussocks of grass, planks of wood, clothes even, a suitcase and travelling-bags. In the distance was Flatsea; it was too far away to detect many separate details, but they could see houses surrounded by water. The island had changed: it was a long narrow spit of land instead of its normal shape, almost as round as a dish.

'I left my wedding-ring on the draining-board,' said Charley.

'That's not all you've lost,' said Doris, in a choked voice.

The engine spluttered and died. Charley got out, opened the bonnet, and frantically dried the plugs. He was ankle-deep in water. Miraculously the car started again; he turned it round and they drove back into Oozedam.

'Where are we going?'

'The nearest phone. We must try and get hold of Martin or Peter. Then the police. They must know what's happening. Then to Ann's, if we can get there, to see if Ron is all right.'

'My God, Charley. To think this can happen. Three of my boys! Where are they? If anything's happened I'll never forgive myself, never!'

'Shut up! Get a grip on yourself!'

Martin's car was the last vehicle to cross the bridge between Flatsea and the mainland. Though the road ran near the sea wall, they saw nothing to alarm them unduly. Water running down the inside of the concrete or lying in pools beside the railway line was unusual but it had happened before; and so had waves booming against the wall, showering spray onto the road. The wind worried them more than the sea. It swung the car towards the hedge, and made the two yellow moons of other cars coming towards them waver unsteadily. There were branches lying in the road as the Oozedam crowd in the pub had said. Martin drove slowly, and was relieved when the first houses and street-lamps appeared.

They could see now how strong this wind was, battering at trees, spinning a closed-open sign at a petrol station round at crazy speed, whirling a cardboard box across the road in front of them. Lights glowed cosily behind curtains where people were watching the Queen, or upstairs in bedrooms and bathrooms. There was no one about; the town was dreary and empty. Oozedam was a grey place at the best of times. It had built its fortunes on fish, and when that trade had dwindled, the car ferries had taken its place. People drove straight to the ship, then embarked for Holland or Denmark and paid no attention to these nondescript East Coast streets.

When they were inside the flat Martin began to feel uneasy again. There *was* something unusually sinister about this wind, the way it whooshed between the attic gables and the chimney pots, smashed the empty milk bottles on people's doorsteps. It even stopped the sound of next door's television penetrating their wall. As he cleaned his teeth he thought he could hear cries, not human, but perhaps the animals in their sheds on the allotments. He opened the curtains, but could see nothing. Then there was a heavy thud and a tearing noise, a large lump of wood it sounded like, hitting a fence. He opened the window. The gale immediately blew the curtains in his face, slammed the door and knocked a plastic mug into the basin. He leaned out, trying to see. The triumphant thunder of the sea sounded very near. He could just make out the line of the railway embankment in the dark, but beyond it nothing. It was one dark mass. Then, as his eyes became used to the blackness, he could see movement out there. Water. Some men running along the railway line. And he could hear above the wind faint screams, pigs probably, frightened by the noise. The sea had come over and was filling up the space between the wall and the embankment. He shut the window with difficulty, and went into the kitchen.

'Ann, the allotments are flooded. Do you think it will come up any further?'

'They've been flooded before. There were some pigs

drowned last year. The Council's always telling people they shouldn't keep animals out there, but nobody takes any notice.'

'Has it ever come over the embankment?'

'Never.'

'That's what I thought.'

'What do you mean?'

'Well ... a first time, perhaps? I'm ... I don't know ...'

'Come on! It would be fantastic if the sea came over! Why, that embankment's been there at least a hundred years!'

There was a crashing rending noise from the roof next door, a moment's silence, then something smashing in pieces.

'A slate.'

Ann shivered. 'Let's go to bed. Or we'll talk ourselves into a panic.'

'Why hot water bottles?' She was holding two.

'It's so cold. I bought them yesterday.'

'You have me.'

When they were in bed they heard a distant muffled boom, not a loud noise, but long and deep as if some enormous heavy thing was being slowly pushed, then a great shout from the sea, a swamping drenching sound of fearsome strength.

'What was it?' she whispered.

'I don't know.'

'I'm frightened now. Hold me.'

'I am.'

They listened. Wind. Sea. Nothing else. The scream of a pig, nearer maybe than it should have been. Then the telephone rang, outside on the downstairs landing.

'Not for us, I hope.'

'Dad? Peter? Ron? I wonder where Ron is.'

Lynwyn, the Jamaican girl downstairs, walked across her room. They heard her answer the phone, then her feet on the stairs.

'Martin. It's your brother.'

'Right, I'm coming.' He rolled out of bed and pulled on his trousers. 'Which brother?'

'I don't know. He says it's urgent.'

He listened to Peter's brief message, his terrified shouts of 'Save me! We're drowning!' and felt sick with fear and guilt.

'Peter! Get out! Get upstairs! Peter?' But the phone was dead.

He rushed back into the flat, shouted to Ann to get dressed, threw his arms into his T-shirt and ran to the wardrobe for a coat, completely forgetting that Peter had asked him to phone the police.

'We should never have left, never. If anything happens to those two kids I'll never forgive myself. Why did you persuade me? No, it's not your fault. It's mine, entirely mine. Where are the car keys? We're going straight back to Flatsea.'

She was dressed now, too. 'How will we get over the bridge?'

'Swim. Try to. I'd bloody well rather drown than not try.'

They ran downstairs. As they were making for the front door it was flung at them, ripped from its hinges by an enormous tree-trunk that had hit it, and a deluge of water poured in. Ann shrieked and ran back up the stairs. Martin hesitated and it surged round him, piercingly cold. The tree remained wedged in the doorway; the door was jammed between the walls of the hall. In seconds the water was up to his waist, helped by a second avalanche that burst in through the back door and the windows of the downstairs kitchen, preceded by a tremendous smashing of glass. The force of the water pushed open the door of the ground floor flat. He struggled towards it. Inside was a young woman and a tiny baby, born there only ten days before.

'Martin! Come back!' Ann screamed. Lynwyn was now on the stairs shouting at him as well.

'Can't you think of anyone but yourself?' he yelled. 'Catch this.' He pulled off his coat, for it was impeding his progress, and threw it at Ann. It missed and floated down the passage. The water was up to his chest, stifling and icy; he could scarcely breathe with the shock of it. It was slimy and felt more like oil than water, being dirty with innumerable substances it had swept before it since it broke in, from pig-sties, gardens, houses.

Now he was almost into the flat, and swimming.

'Kathleen! Are you all right?'

Then the electricity failed. It was pitch dark.

Part Two
Rescue

Peter struggled towards the kitchen. The water was up to his neck, the cold of it stupefying. When he tried to swim he was pushed back by the force of the torrent against the wood of the staircase. He clung to the banisters. His head felt as if it didn't belong to him and the muscles of his chest seemed rigid as if they were trying to stop his lungs taking in air. Several things banged into him. It was so dark that he was not sure what they were, but he thought they came from the kitchen, the plastic bread-bin, a milk jug. From the bar came the jingling brittle sound of dozens of bottles all crashing into each other. Then the flood began to lose its strength; the flow slackened and it was rising more slowly. He swam towards what he thought was the kitchen door, and banged his head on the wood of its frame. There was still some space between the water and the ceiling, but he was afraid it would not be there for long. He lashed out with one arm trying to find the lintel and hit a cup and saucer floating on the surface, the saucepan he had used earlier to make the cocoa. Then his right foot struck the door-knob, and he was able to heave himself up onto the top of the door, his foot still on the handle, his head touching the ceiling.

'Susan! Where are you?' he shouted.

'Here!' Her voice was quite near him. 'I thought you'd ... I climbed on the table, then pulled a chair onto it. Now I'm standing on the chair.'

'But ... why are you so near me?'

'The sea's pushed the table against the wall and jammed it against something. It's not floating; perhaps it's my weight.'

'We must get out. There won't be much air left soon.'

'How can we?'

'Swim of course. Can you follow me?'

'I can't swim.'

'Bloody hell!' He kicked out from the door with his left foot, and found the table; he stood on it and was holding her thin, wet, shivering body against him. The shock of this for a second was more than his fear or the intense cold. He said 'I'm going to turn round. Put your arms round me, under my armpits. That's right. I'm going to take a very deep breath, then I'm going to swim. Will you trust me?'

'Yes.'

But once in the water the combined weight of both of them dragged him under. She let go of him in fright, then grabbed him round the neck. He was suffocating; her arms were strangling him, and there was water flooding into his mouth and nose. Striking out through the filthy black water from the kitchen table to the staircase were moments very close to death : blinding stars in his eyes and red hot spears in his lungs; he was drowning, here in his own hall, where he had walked unconcerned half an hour ago, or crawled as a baby : he had a sudden picture of himself as a small child on this floor only a foot or so below him, playing with toy bricks. Then he was touching the staircase, groping for the banisters, and heaving himself upwards with an immense effort; her grip loosened as she too grasped one of the uprights, and they were both safe, panting, spitting, spluttering. Then over the top and onto the stairs, and crawling up them, and flopping onto the landing carpet which was dry and infinitely soft, her hand in his and she whispered 'Thank you, thank you, thank you,' and he was kissing her, several times and with a sort of wild exhilaration; and thinking, you don't ask, it happens. He smiled: why for him when the whole world was drowning, and pulling them down with it?

Then he stood up, so weak at the knees he had to lean against the wall in case he fell over, and said in a hoarse whisper, for he had not the strength to speak louder, 'Where are the candles?'

'On your parents' bed.'

He managed shakily to light one, and returned to the landing where she was still sitting. He looked at her in the flickering candlelight; she was soaked, shivering, and exhausted. He thought he had never seen her face, really seen it, till now.

'We nearly drowned,' he said.

'Yes. Yes. But we're safe.'

'If we don't freeze to death.'

He went into the bathroom and started to run hot water into the bath.

'You go in it,' he said. 'Take those clothes off and I'll find some of Mum's.'

She giggled. 'I could get three of me into her things.'

'Well ... how about my jeans? Yes, I've a clean pair, and some vests and pants and sweaters.' He lit another candle and went into his bedroom. 'Don't let the water out when you've finished; as the electricity's gone, the tank will fill up cold. I'll go in it when I come back.' How ordinary this conversation sounded, he thought; it should somehow be important, significant. He put the clothes on the bathroom chair.

'Where are you going?'

'Down to the bar. I'm going to rescue Martin's picture.'

'Peter! You're mad!'

'Get in the bath.'

She did as he told her, and he walked down the stairs into the water. The bottles and glasses in the bar were bobbing and circling and making music, hundreds of sugar-plum fairies. The level had gone down slightly : it was now lower than the top of the bar door. The height had fallen as it spread out across the island, and some of it was making its way out of the pub by the doorways and windows it had burst open. He had no trouble in finding the picture and lifting it off its hook; he slipped his arm through the cord and swam back. On the stairs he found a quart bottle of beer, one of the old-fashioned sort with a stopper, and he took this up with him. He could hear Susan in the bath. He dried the picture with the counterpane from his parents' bed, and stood it on the dressing-table. In the candlelight it seemed unharmed by the salt water, and beautiful. There was all of Martin in it. Then he took off his wet clothes and slipped under his parents' huge eiderdown, and waited for Susan to finish. Outside King Charles's head moaned in the wind. He began to feel the shock. Now that he was a little warmer, a huge wave of relief that filled him and demanded release almost wanted to break all the bones in his body in order to wash over him and swallow him up.

Susan came out of the bathroom.

'All right?' he murmured wearily.

'Yes. I put lots of cold in it. The heat seemed to scald me, because I was so frozen, I think.'

The sense of relaxation unwound him more and more as he lay in the bath; his whole body was tingling and melting; he was a disembodied spirit, dead, nothing but a voice or a ghost. He almost fell asleep.

Later, when he had dressed, he drank some of the beer, not

much, for it made him feel sick. He remembered the brandy.

'Susan. Do you want some of this?'

'No thanks. Come and look.' She was standing by the window in Martin's old room. The clouds had lifted and the moon was shining, its brilliance dazzling on the sea with a strange cold intensity, illuminating everything. There were black and silver trees and houses, all marooned in the sea, not a blade of grass anywhere.

A light waved in a window about fifty yards away.

'It's Mum and Dad! Peter, how can we tell them we're safe?'

'Put the candle on the window-sill. No! I've a better idea! Dad keeps a torch in his bedroom.' He went off to fetch it.

'What are you going to do?'

'Send a message. Does your Dad understand Morse?'

'Yes, I think so. Yes, he learned it in the war.'

'I was a scout for two years. The only thing they taught me was the Morse code. I wonder if I can remember it.'

Slowly he spelled out the message, 'We are safe. Peter. Susan.' Back came the answer, after what seemed an eternity of slowness, 'Thank God'. Then the torch in the Allgoods' window whirled and leaped in a joyous dance. Peter sent another message. 'We are alone. Mum and Dad not returned. Martin and Ann left before it happened. Ron not come home.' The Allgoods' torch began to spell out an answer.

'What's he saying?' Susan asked.

'Wrap ... up ... well ... keep ... each ... other ... warm.'

They both laughed. 'Roger and out,' Peter flashed.

'It's cold in here,' said Susan.

'This is Martin's room. Was.' It was the smallest bedroom, now full of spare furniture and junk. The only things of

67

Martin's were three cardboard boxes full of odds and ends. They went into Peter's bedroom, and sat on the floor, their backs against the bed, close together for warmth inside his eiderdown and the patchwork quilt he had brought back from Grandma's. It smelled of mothballs, old and cosy and secure.

'Do you want some of this brandy now?'

'A sip.'

They took a mouthful each from the bottle, and choked almost as much as when they pulled themselves from the water.

'This is a decadent teenage party,' said Peter. 'Mum was reading about them in the *Sunday People* this morning. Drinking spirits, and a girl in my bedroom.'

'Peter, please take me out to the disco. I do want to.'

'Yes. The soonest we can.'

He put his arm round her, and after a while she fell asleep against his shoulder. He was happy, a soaring, liberating sensation, free like flying weightless through the air, like nothing he had ever known. Absurd, he thought, with my father's house a wreck, and the rest of the family Heaven knew where or in what trouble. He took another sip of brandy, and stared round at his room, the blank walls papered pink, the wardrobe, the chest of drawers. There's nothing in here, he thought, that says it's me, not like Ron's, cluttered with things. I shall put some of Martin's pictures up. He felt drowsy, and tried to sleep, but could not. Susan began to be a weight on his arm; he stirred, and she woke.

He shivered, not with the cold, but the happiness could not last. Nagging questions the first shock of everything had swept out of his mind crept back. Where *were* Mum and Dad? David had said they'd gone. Returned to his house?

Surely they were all right. Martin — safe from the flood, he knew that, but his phone call must have driven his brother crazy with worry. What was Martin doing? Trying to rescue him, in terrible difficulties that were completely unnecessary as he was quite safe? And Ron. Anything could have happened to him, hard though it was to imagine the god-like Aaron really suffering. And his grandparents: they would surely have been in bed, and therefore unharmed. He stood up and went to the window. He could see the end of their cottage, but whether there was a light there or not he couldn't be certain; the angle of the windows obscured it. All the familiar things looked unreal as in a dream, the flickering of the guttering candle making his room insubstantial, the hard unnatural sheen of the moon on the water turning trees and houses into cardboard cut-outs.

'What's the matter?'

'I'm worried. Worried stiff now I think about it. Where's Ron? And what's happened to Grandpa and Grandma? I'm ashamed I didn't think of it before. What's Martin doing?'

Susan came to the window. 'The water's gone down.'

'Yes. A little. I think ... I ought to try and get to my grandparents.'

'But it will still be freezing cold!'

'Well, I'm going to try. I wonder ... I think there's a pair of flippers somewhere in Ron's cupboard.'

They went into Aaron's room. Susan exclaimed in surprise. There were clothes thrown about everywhere, a guitar on the bed, the walls covered in pictures — pop groups, motor bikes, naked women, Aaron playing football, Aaron playing his guitar at the last school dance surrounded by admirers.

'It's a wonder your Mum allows it.'

'They had a row when he started pinning up nudes. She

69

said she wouldn't clean in here any more and she hasn't. Ron does it all himself.'

'Not very well either.'

He could not find the flippers. Across a chair lay a pair of trousers Aaron had dropped there, the legs sprawled out flat. Peter picked them up and put them away: the sight was too disturbing; they looked somehow dead.

He undressed to his underclothes and went down the stairs. The water came up to his shoulders. Its cold was still almost unbearable.

'I think I'll be able to wade through.'

'Wait. I'm coming with you.'

'What for?'

'If we can get through I'd best go home to Mum and Dad.'

'All right.' He felt disappointed.

He held her hand and they struggled through to her parents' house. The scene around them was quite extraordinary. Most of the island was quite drowned, and the surface of the water, now calmer, like a sea of ice in the moonlight. Pieces of wood floated by, plastic cups and bottles, dead chickens. A cat, in the ash tree, was mewing pitifully.

'Good night, Susan.' He kissed her.

'I'll come down to see you in the morning as soon as it's possible.'

His grandparents' door, too, was open, and downstairs was a now familiar scene of floating household objects. He could hear Grandma reading aloud, a monotonous unending drone.

'Grandma! Where are you? It's me, Peter.'

'In bed!'

He found the stairs and went up. His muscles were shuddering with uncontrollable spasms. They were both in bed, peering at him over the tops of their spectacles. There was one candle, on Grandma's side. Grandpa looked glum.

'I can't sleep,' he grumbled. 'All this damned moonlight. And she will go on and on reading. Corinthians, all that bit about charity.'

'Dry yourself, boy,' said Grandma. 'There's a towel on that rail. What have you done with your clothes?'

'Never seen anything like it and I'm eighty-five. Much worse than '97. Much worse. Are you all right?'

'Yes. But I'm on my own. Susan's quite safe; she's at home now. Martin and Ann are back at the flat, but there's no sign of Mum and Dad or Ron.'

'They'll survive,' said Grandma. 'We must trust in God.'

'Is that God's work?' asked Grandpa angrily.

'Maybe. We don't know, do we? He sent a flood once before, you remember.'

'Humph. You may know your Bible, Bessy, but you don't know everything.'

'I'll go back,' said Peter, irritated by their complete lack of any sense of reality.

'Go back?' cried Grandma. 'What nonsense! You stay here. There's sheets and blankets on the spare-room bed, and I'll find you a pair of Fred's pyjamas.'

'No. There's nobody else to look after the pub.'

He went downstairs and pushed his way through the water. 'He's a good lad, that one,' he heard Grandpa say. A dead horse lay on its side against a tree. Candles and storm-lanterns were alight in the windows of all the houses; it looked like Christmas. Back at home he dried himself, then sipped more brandy; and feeling enormously tired, he curled up in his bed and slept.

*

Aaron roused himself at last from his misery. He knew that if he did not stir and attempt to keep warm he might never be able to move again. There was hardly any feeling in his legs or hands; they were insensible blocks of ice. Other people sat on the roof, huddled together or stood, stamping their feet and flailing their arms, trying to keep some heat in their bodies. He decided to walk along to the front of the train to see what had happened. Someone spoke to him, but he answered curtly, hardly hearing the question. The man was trying to make a list of names, of survivors as well as those missing. Aaron eventually told him who he was, and the name of his friend.

'Anyone else in your compartment?'

'No.'

'I think that's everybody accounted for. But I'm afraid there's ten drowned in there.' He pointed to where the over-turned first carriage lay under the sea.

'Is this your jacket I'm wearing?'

'Yes.'

'Take it. I'm going to swim for it.'

'I think we should all try that, those of us who can. But not yet. The sea's far too strong.'

Aaron thrust the jacket at him, and made his way back to John. He knelt beside him, touched the dead boy's hands and face, then unclasped the Christopher medal, and fastened it round his own neck. Numb though he was physically, he had never before felt such strong emotion. He remembered his remark to John 'I've never had a chance to love anybody', and he knew it was a lie. He jumped into the sea.

He was so deadened with cold that it was no worse than being on the train roof, but fear that the sea would take him too made him thrash out furiously with his arms and legs; it was so rough that every movement was a struggle to keep his head above the water as one soaking saturating weight of a wave after another rained down on his head. The current pulled him sideways, then back against the train; he kicked himself free, and his arms were round a telegraph pole. The sea tried to suck him back, but he held onto the wood, and as the wave surged forwards he let go and he could feel earth underfoot, slippery and impossible to grip, and he slid, swallowing the foul, slimy water, under the surface; then another wave threw him into a wire fence. He clutched at this, and forced himself over it; then a huge wave swept him headlong inland and he couldn't breathe at all, he couldn't push his head up through it, he would burst, he was getting more feeble, this was the end ... he cracked his head against a tree. With his last strength he grabbed at a branch and heaved himself upwards. The moonlight showed him that the tree was in a corner of a field, and though the land beyond was flooded, the hedge was acting for the moment as a breakwater taking the full fury of the sea. On the far side it was calmer. He drank in lungfuls of air, almost doubling up with the pain in his chest, his heart racing madly. The wind was swaying his perch dangerously, and he crawled out along a branch, noticing dimly that there was blood on his arm and that his legs were filthy with mud and dirt from the tree-trunk. He dropped into the water on the other side; it was not so deep, coming up only to his shoulders, but it was treacherous underfoot, slithery ridges and furrows of ploughed earth. In the distance was dry land. He walked, floundering and falling for a yard, then swam. It was easier this time, though he was nearly exhausted and very slow. There was a terrible pain as something stabbed into his left thigh, and his head went under in a half-somersault as it abruptly stopped him swimming any further. He came up retching, then stood – the water was only waist-high – but he was still caught. He fumbled desperately with both hands, forcing his leg back, and it came free suddenly with another jab of pain. It was barbed wire. He forced it downwards as far as he could, groping for a place to hold where there were no barbs, and floated himself over. Now he walked as the water became shallower, and finally he was out of it, stumbling through a field of cabbages.

Through the gate and into a lane, where the stones were sharp and agonizing to his feet, but it led to a road with the first houses of Oozedam and a pavement to walk on. He dragged himself along. His main fear now was that his strength might give out before he reached Martin's. Blood was pouring from the cut in his thigh and mingling with the mud on his legs, and it throbbed dully, but he would not allow it to stop him. These were the only thoughts in his head; get to Martin's; leg won't stop me. He was beyond noticing the wind's power to freeze him still further; he was so numb that he could not have said whether he felt cold or hot. Nor did it occur to him that there were now rather more people about than would normally be expected, running purposefully or in alarm. People stared and asked if he was all right, and he nodded, or muttered 'I'm going to my brother's. I'm O.K.' and after looking at him strangely, they left him with some reluctance, having desperate worries of their own to see to. Even a policeman who stopped him let him go on.

'I'm standing on the bed! Over here! Quick!'
Martin was swept by the current towards Kathleen, and

hit something soft and wet and heavy on the surface of the water which span away from him.

'That's Donna!' she screamed. 'Oh my God! What have you done? That was her mattress; I was holding it up!' She moved towards him, scrabbling frantically. He gripped her hands and held them away from him.

He let go of her, and knocked into a piece of wood and a shoe that was still floating, then became entwined in a sheet that draped itself round his face, cold and smothering. He sank right under the water as he disentangled himself. He was coughing and choking and thought he would sink again, but there was the top of the wardrobe door, and he clung on to it until he recovered. He struck out again and found the mattress, water-logged, just below the surface, but the baby was there, and apparently still asleep.

'I've got her!'

'Where is she?'

'I'm going to swim out, pushing the mattress.'

'What shall I do?'

'Swim for your life!'

The mattress was cumbersome and not easy to guide. He wondered how long his strength would last. He was a good swimmer, but his muscles were knotting painfully with shock, and his breath was coming in short, painful jerks. He found the doorway, but the water had risen above it. There was only one thing to do: abandon the mattress, and plunge underneath the lintel with the baby in his arms. As he rose above the surface in the hall she began to scream with terror. He swam to the stairs, where Ann and Lynwyn were standing holding candles. He thrust the baby into Lynwyn's arms. He was speechless. They ran up the stairs, and he followed slowly. They were in Lynwyn's room, taking off Donna's wet clothes and drying her.

'She's a darling,' said Ann, trying to soothe her.

'Where's Kathleen?' Lynwyn asked.

Martin turned. 'What? . . . She was supposed to be following me!' And he ran out, back down the stairs into the water. He found the lintel of the door with some difficulty and ducked under.

'Kathleen!'

'I can't find the door! I'm almost touching the ceiling! Where are you?'

'Over here! Follow the direction of my voice! I'm not coming back in or we might never find the way out.'

He could hear her splashing, but it seemed ages before she was near him. His foot touched her face.

'Hold my hand. I'm going to duck under and pull you after me.'

'No, I can't. I can't . . .' Her words were lost as he dragged her under. When they surfaced on the other side of the doorway, she gasped. 'You shouldn't have done that! I've swallowed so much water!'

'If you hadn't you'd have bloody well drowned!'

When he had taken off his wet clothes, he sat down on the bed feeling faint. He was breathing as if he had run a mile; every part of his body was trembling and would not stop. He had never felt so cold in all his life.

He dried himself and dressed, putting on two thick sweaters. He walked slowly down to Lynwyn's room. Kathleen was wearing some of Lynwyn's clothes; she was nursing Donna, who had quietened down to a good steady cry instead of the first strident screeches of terror.

'Is she all right?'

'Yes. None the worse for it, I think.'

Ann came in from the kitchen. 'Martin, the gas won't

light. You turn on the tap, and it makes a funny noise. There's no gas coming out.'

'The water must be in the pipes. Better not try; it might be dangerous.'

'But that means we can't cook anything or heat our-selves!'

'I've a little camping stove with a bottle of gas,' said Lynwyn.

'Let's all go upstairs,' said Martin. 'We've got a paraffin heater, so we can at least keep warm. How's the oil?'

'Enough for an hour or two.'

'Good. We'll pull it out from the grate, and light a fire as well. We've got paper, and we can burn that old rickety chair in the kitchen. One of the surfboards is wood. And the frames from my canvases.'

'Martin, you mustn't do that!'

'Well, we'll see ... Now, we'd better look at the water. It may still be rising.'

As far as they could make out in the dim candlelight it had gone down slightly. Lynwyn, however, did not feel safe in her flat, and they moved her mattress and bedding up-stairs, her clothes and some of her other possessions. Ann lit a fire; the baby was quiet; all three women were busy with various jobs.

'I'm going, then,' said Martin.

'Where to?'

'To find Peter.' Ann looked at him. Martin smiled faintly. 'I'll be back, don't worry. Thank God I've got the wet suit.' He took it from the wardrobe, and changed into it. 'I'm taking the malibu.'

'You look like a frogman,' said Kathleen.

'That's just about what I am.'

'How will you get there?' Ann asked.

'Walk where I can. Ride the malibu. Steal a boat. I don't know. But I've got to try, Ann.'

'Yes.' She looked pale and very frightened. He took her in his arms and kissed her. 'Do take care,' she said, trying to make it sound light, and she stroked his face. 'Martin, I couldn't ...' He broke away from her and left. On the first floor landing he thought he would see if the telephone was working. There was no dialling tone, only a distant babble of voices, as if dozens of wires had become inextricably mixed up.

He had to swim across the street, propelling the malibu in front of him. Cold water trickled between the rubber suit and his skin. The flood he could see had risen to the height of the first floor of the houses, but had fallen back a little leaving seaweed and wisps of grass hanging from some bedroom window-sills. The wind whipped across the surface of the water. There were candles in most of the bedroom windows, shadows of people behind them, faces looking out. In Pretoria Street he reached dry land.

He walked through the side-streets in the direction of the main road to Flatsea, the malibu under his arm. The water inside his suit was now warmer, less uncomfortable. There were several people about, hurrying in all directions, but most of them stopped to ask him for information, and tell him what they knew. A family of ten were trapped in a basement in Canewdon Road ... the harbourmaster was stranded on the roof of his office ... the fire station was under water and all of its appliances out of action ... the landlord of The Grove Tavern had drowned in his cellar ... the hospital was badly damaged, but there were no casualties ... four people were known to have died in Elsie Street, one of them a girl of five ... A police car drove slowly along, broadcasting a warning to people not to turn on gas fires or stoves. A woman ran by, saying 'A damn fine night for surfing!'

He made his way out of the town through streets that were mostly dry; only occasionally was there water, and that no more than knee-height. Three times he was asked for help, but he refused, hating himself for doing so, but Peter was his first priority. He did not dare think too much about his youngest brother. The chances of finding him alive might only be slim. Yet Peter was sensible, a good swimmer; he may even have got out in time. Even if the water was upstairs in the pub he could be in the loft. But those last words on the phone, 'Save me! Save me! We're drowning!' and the terrible panic in his voice perhaps meant things had happened just too quickly ...

The moon was out now and he could see his way clearly. His difficulties started when he came near the wrecked train. The water here was up to his throat at times; he had to swim, and this was not easy, for the sea was churning violently backwards and forwards, as if it was breaking on a beach. He could see people crowded together on the roof of the train; it must be Aaron's train, and he yelled 'Ron!' several times, but nobody heard. The wind was blowing in the wrong direction. He wondered whether he ought to try and struggle over there, but decided not to; either Ron was on the roof, or ... But this was the same situation as Peter was in. He was either safe, or dead. Neither of them could be swimming now; neither, he suddenly realized, in fact needed his help. But he went on. Aaron was older than Peter and easily the strongest of the four brothers; if Peter could somehow be rescued, then they would go back to Ron.

Soon he could see Flatsea clearly, what was left of it;

there was the roof of The King's Head sharp and silver
against the sky. There was about half a mile of water between him and Peter. He lay on the malibu and paddled with
his hands. The waves were rough, but no rougher here
on the submerged land than he had ridden over last summer
at Newquay; out away to his left in the open sea they were
impossible; he could hear the thunder of the surf and see
the hungry tumbling of the foam, a greenish white in the
moonlight. The wall, despite the breaches in it, still acted as
some kind of barrier here, and kept the force of the main
body of the sea away. He paddled on, the wet suit stopping
him from becoming stiff and numb. He sang to keep his
spirits up:

'Following the north star brings us back to harbour;
Warm winds are blowing back across the sea!
Rock gently, sailboat, rock us all to sleep!'
Here in the sailboat no one can discover;

Aaron was reeling like a drunk, gripping railings, pausing
for moments to gather strength, his leg muscles about to
seize up, telling his brain they were going to give out at any
moment and buckle under. Downhill, down Pretoria Street,
and there was Martin's road, Balaclava Street. It was under
water. It was too much to bear, and he collapsed. The street-
lights were not working, but in the moonlight, a man who
was swimming through the flood saw him fall.

'Can you get up, son?'

'No,' he whispered. 'I'm all in. Take me over the water.
Sixty-four Balaclava Street.'

'You should be in hospital.'

'No. Brother's.'

'If I could get you to hospital I would, but there's not a
chance. Eight feet of it there on the ground floor.' He picked

Aaron up, muttering with surprise at his weight, and struggled back into the water. 'Sixty-four, was it? That's the one with the tree wedged in the door.'

Somehow they scrambled over this obstacle, and were through the hall and up the stairs.

'What's your brother's name?'

'Martin.'

'Martin!!' Ann came running out of the flat, Lynwyn and Kathleen behind her. 'Get this lad into bed at once; he's very ill. For God's sake get him warm or he'll die. And do something about that cut leg.'

Aaron, now only dimly aware of what was going on, felt himself being handed over and the women were placing him gently on the carpet; the air was thick and warm, almost intolerably stuffy; they were pulling his underpants down – they shouldn't be doing that, but perhaps it didn't matter any more; he was being dried with towels; the voices murmured around him; their hands were gentle and healing. Women.

'He's handsome.'

'That's bleeding badly. It's very deep.'

'Warm water and cotton wool.'

'Elastoplast? On the shelf.'

'This piece will do for his cheekbone.'

'Too young for us. Or maybe not.'

'I've refilled the hot water bottles.'

'Waxy. Could be frostbite.'

'No hot water bottles then. It could be dangerous, I think.'

Martin, where was he? There was the rim of a glass between his lips, whisky; he was being sick. They were dressing him in clean clothes, lifting him; he was in bed.

'John's ... drowned,' he managed to say, thickly, and an enormous pressure rose from inside him which he couldn't

81

resist, making his eyes dissolve the room into whirling yellow shapes, and it hit his brain like a sledgehammer, and he knew nothing more.

Charley ran from the telephone kiosk to the car. 'I can't get through on that one either. That's the third – it can't be vandals, not three in a row. I reckon the telephone exchange has been damaged.'

'What do we do now?' asked Doris.

'Go to the police.'

The police station was well away from the flooded area, but it was obvious when they arrived there that a major catastrophe had occurred. A young constable was on duty behind the desk, looking tired and harassed, trying to answer questions and take information from a crowd of agitated people, some of them on the verge of panic. It was difficult to move, for so much miscellaneous luggage was cluttering up the room : suitcases, cardboard boxes, people's pets – three cages with budgerigars; several cats and dogs; there was even a pig tied to a door handle. A senior officer appeared and ordered two of his men to move everything out to the Ferry Primary School; 'It's like a zoo in here,' he said. Messages were shouted from one official to another; policemen dashed in and out; all was pandemonium and disorder.

Charley and Doris waited, learning from the conversation some details of what had happened. Doris was very relieved to hear that the patients in the hospital were safe; only the ground floor had had to be evacuated.

'Get the caretaker at the Methodist Church to open the hall ... I don't care if he's in bed or not ... I want him to take in a hundred people ...'

'Ask the W.V.S. to do three hundred soups immediately. No? Oh, no electricity –'

'An old lady in Royal Street wants to know if we can find her dog. Answers to the name of Holly.'

'The Yacht Club say they've no more space.'

'Get those bloody cats out of here!'

'At least ten breaches in our patch. The worst one's knocked out the power station. Concrete blocks from the wall have smashed all the equipment.'

'Warn Southend.'

'The Town Clerk's in his office right now, sir. The Mayor's at a dinner party in Harwich.'

Doris spotted a constable she knew, who occasionally came to The King's Head for a pint when he was off duty. Charley pushed his way through the crowd and managed to stop the man just as he was hurrying out. From him he learned that most of Flatsea was under water, but as far as the police knew the sea had not reached the first floor of any of the houses. However, it would be impossible to rescue anybody before dawn. 'You'd scarcely believe it, Charley,' he said, 'but there's a chronic shortage of small boats. Here we are living right by the sea, but because it's January most of the dinghies and small craft are unseaworthy – caulking, repairs. And those that were outside have been smashed to pieces.' Charley, thinking now that Peter and Martin were probably safe upstairs in the pub, maybe even asleep, decided that Aaron was their major worry, and asked the constable if he knew whether the last train had reached Flatsea before the sea burst in. He now learned of the train's derailment, that a number of people were missing, and that a party of sea scouts had gone out to try and rescue the survivors.

Charley went white. 'I've good reason to think my son Ron was on that train,' he said. 'Don't tell Doris.'

'Go down to the Comprehensive,' said the constable. 'That's where they'll take them. There'll be a list of names.'

He rejoined Doris, and told her most of what he had heard, though saying only about Aaron that if he had been stranded in Oozedam he might be at the school.

'What are we waiting for?' she demanded. 'Come on.'

The school hall was an enormous area which easily accommodated fifteen hundred children at morning assembly. Now it was lit by dozens of candles and for once looked beautiful rather than functional, a vast cavern, its roof lost in the leaping shadows. People were milling about everywhere. Many were already asleep, or trying to sleep, on makeshift bedding on the floor; others, half-dressed, hurried about looking for washrooms, or other members of their families. Some children were crying and adults were attempting to comfort them, while others ran about in a great state of excitement, enjoying the novelty of it all. The headmaster darted here and there with lists in his hand, answering questions, directing people. His secretary had moved her desk and typewriter into the hall and was busy taking particulars of new arrivals, who came in every minute, many of them dazed, drenched and hysterical.

Charley joined the queue at her desk, while Doris buttonholed the headmaster. At last it was his turn. Yes, the survivors from the train had all arrived. She checked through her list. Aaron's name was not on it.

Charley stared, unable to speak for a few seconds. He took out his handkerchief and wiped his eyes.

'Aaron Brown, believed missing,' she said.

'Don't say that. You know him, my Ron? In the sixth form.'

'Yes. I ... I don't ... I can't say how ... Wait a minute!'
She shuffled through the papers on her desk. 'I have another
list. One of the men rescued from the train wrote everybody's names down. I'll just check it. Yes, his name *is* on
the list! How very odd! Why isn't he here? Just like him.'

Charley's relief left him as drained as the anguish of a
moment before had done. He wiped his eyes again. He
thought for a moment that he was going to pass out. 'He's
probably gone to his brother's,' he murmured. He moved
away, but the secretary called him back.

'Mr Brown! One moment. You're from Flatsea, aren't
you?'

'Yes.'

'You can't go back there tonight.'

'I know, I ...'

'What are you going to do?'

'I don't know. Go to my son David's. I haven't really
thought.'

'You're an evacuee, you know, just like everyone else.'

'Am I? Yes, I suppose I am.' It had not occurred to him
until that moment that he was also homeless, and now
Authority wanted to know all the particulars, where Peter
and Martin were – 'I remember Martin,' said the secretary,
'nice polite boy. Prefect' – where David lived, how long he
would be likely to stay with David, and so on. Just like the
war, Charley thought, just like the blitz : we escaped all that
living on the island. Now it's caught up with us. Even lost
my wedding-ring.

'What now?' Doris asked, when they were outside.

'We'll go and see if he's at Ann's. We won't be able to get
to the flat, because the road's eight feet under water, or so
Bill Masters said at the police station. But we may be able
to see from the rise in Pretoria Street if there's any light on.'

'That headmaster. Who does he think he is? Says Ron's a most unsatisfactory boy. Never settled down properly to serious work. Too much pop music, too much sport, he said. Waste of a fine intelligence. I said the boy's got to relax sometimes! I told him.'

In Ann's flat the curtains were open. They could see a candle burning, and shadows behind it, caused by someone moving.

'He's there, he's there!' Charley shouted at the top of his voice. '*Ron!*'

'It might only be Ann and Martin.'

'But they're at the pub. Ron! *Ron!*'

'Charley! Don't shout like that!'

'How else can we make him hear? We can't get through that water unless you want to swim.'

'Throw something at the window.'

He found a stone, but it missed. His second throw, however, hit the glass. Someone lifted the window. Ann.

'Ann!' Charley shouted. 'Are you all right? Is Ron with you?'

'Yes! We're safe; he's here.'

'Thank God,' Doris murmured.

'And Martin? Is he there too?'

'Gone back to the pub to look for Peter.'

'Peter! What's wrong?'

Ann thought it unwise to mention the phone call. 'Nothing. Martin wanted to make sure Peter wasn't in any danger. He'll be back soon. Are you coming over?'

'No. We'll go back to David's and wait till the water's gone down a bit. Look after yourselves.'

Ann waved and shut the window. Charley put his arms round Doris. 'I thought he was drowned! Now everything's all right!'

'It isn't. What about Peter?'

The flood in The King's Head came up to Martin's chest, but the moonlight showed him that at its highest it had nearly reached the ceiling. There was a dirty line above the picture rail, and wet silt and mud smeared on the walls. He had no idea of the time – the clock in the kitchen had stopped when the electricity failed – but he guessed it must now be well after midnight. The bar looked as if it had been wrecked in a fight: tables and chairs had been thrown against one wall and most of them were smashed beyond repair. There was broken glass everywhere, but he found a bottle of rum that was undamaged. He unscrewed the top and drank from it.

There was no sign of a body, so, leaving the malibu on the counter like a stranded whale, he went upstairs. Peter was fast asleep in bed. Martin touched him: he was warm and breathing. The cold wet sensation made Peter stir.

'What is it? Who's there?'

'Martin.'

'Martin!' Peter sat upright. 'I thought it might be Ron. How did you get here? Wait a second; I'll light a candle.' He groped his way out of bed, and a moment later the two brothers could see each other.

'I paddled over on the malibu.'

'You must be frozen. There's some brandy there.'

'You've drunk all that? Dad will have a fit.'

'Susan had a little.'

'Susan? Where is she?'

'She's all right. She's at home. And the old people are safe. I swam up there.'

'I expected to find two drowned corpses.'

'I know, the phone call. I'm sorry.' And Peter explained

87

what had happened. Then Martin told him what he knew of the situation in Oozedam, and said that Peter should come back with him, and their grandparents too; it would be much safer than staying on the island; they could all go to David's; the water level was only going down because the breaches in the wall must be huge, and that meant the next high tide would swamp the island again. Peter thought the idea was ridiculous.

'Why?' asked Martin, irritated, knowing that his younger brother was right. But he did not want his arduous journey to prove completely pointless. If only he had not listened to Peter and trusted his own judgement instead! Probably neither of them would have got wet at all, and they could be fast asleep now, in warm beds.

'Why don't you take that thing off and dry yourself?'

'If I do that I shall never get back, and Ann will be insane with fright. Now listen, Peter. I insist you come back with me.'

'How, for a start?'

'I could find a boat.' He knew this sounded absurd.

Peter just laughed. 'I'm certainly not going to swim, or even wade. I've had enough cold water for one night.'

'Well, how are you going to cope with the next high tide?'

'Ah. I've got that all worked out. I've set Dad's alarm clock for five o'clock. It's about low tide then and I reckon the water will all have gone. First job, get as much sand as I can possibly find and fill those sacks in the shed. Block up all the doorways with sandbags except one, as the customers will have to get in somehow —'

'Customers! Now you're being ridiculous. Who do you think's coming out here to drink tomorrow?'

'It doesn't matter if no one comes. The law says the pub

has to be open every day of the year except Christmas Day. I shall keep plenty of sandbags in the bar for the front door when the tide comes. I'm going to nail wood over the broken windows. I'm going to clean out that bar –'

'Enough work for a week. And where are you going to find the sand?'

'There's plenty in the shed. Dad bought some last week to do some concreting out the back.' He yawned. 'Now let me go to sleep. Oh, and Susan will be down first thing to help.'

'Will she?'

'I saved your picture. I swam through the bar and brought it upstairs and dried it.'

'Peter, you're marvellous. And I thought I was the great hero, coming out here like this.'

'You are. But I'm sorry I made you.'

'So long, landlord. If I find Dad first I'll tell him he has no worries.'

'Aren't you going to look at the picture?'

'It will keep. Are you quite sure Grandma's all right?'

'Yes. It's Ron I'm scared about.'

'Yes. But he has nine lives.' Martin decided not to say anything about the wrecked train; there was no point in upsetting Peter unnecessarily.

'He's used up eight.'

'He's probably staying at John Hewitt's.' Martin took a long swig of brandy, then started out on the journey back. There was no sign of anyone on or near the train, and on the dry road beyond it a police car that had come out to rescue an elderly couple in a flooded bungalow stopped beside him. The driver offered him a lift. Martin, who was now beginning to feel very tired, accepted gratefully. The malibu had to be left in the bungalow as there was no room for it in the car. He explained what he had been doing, and was listened to with great interest; this was the first news the police had had of conditions on Flatsea from someone who had been on the island, and it was immediately relayed over the radio to headquarters.

'We'll get a team of men over there at breakfast time,' said the policeman. 'I think we may have to evacuate everyone until the walls are repaired.'

'That may take weeks!'

'Yes. Oh, they'll be all right; we're opening up several rescue centres. They'll be well looked after. The main problem at the moment is a shortage of blankets, but there should be a lorry-load from Cambridge during the morning.'

'My brother's not going to like that!'

'Beggars can't be choosers,' said the old man, who was sitting in the back. It was the first time he had spoken since leaving his home. His wife stared ahead, a glazed frightened expression on her face. She could not stop shivering.

'What's happened to the passengers on the train?' Martin asked.

'They've been rescued. But there are several missing or dead.'

'My brother Ron may well have been on that train.'

'You ought to stay the rest of the night at the school. Your brother will be there. That's where I'm taking these two. Balaclava Street is still flooded; the railway embankment's holding the water in.'

'I must get back to my girlfriend. She'll be terrified out of her mind.'

'Love is stronger than water, is it?'

'Neither can the floods drown it,' Martin said, and laughed. 'So the Bible tells us.'

'It ain't necessarily so,' said the policeman, turning the car into Pretoria Street.

At about two o'clock in the morning Grandma announced that she was going downstairs to cook breakfast.

'At this hour of the night!' exclaimed Fred. 'What's got into you, girl?'

'I'm hungry.' She started to dress. 'Give me your matches.'

He stared at her in amazement, and slowly shook his head. 'After all these years not a day passes without you causing miracles. You be careful with that there gas. If the water's in it it might be dangerous.'

'It's only Calor gas.'

'Makes no difference. What are you putting your clothes on for? You'll get them wet.'

'Fred Brown, you don't think I'm going down to my kitchen in the nude? The idea!' She jammed her hat on, and thrust the pin firmly into it. 'Matches, Fred.'

'In my coat pocket, over there. And who's going to see you, girl?'

'That's not the point, and if you can't see the point at your age you ought to be ashamed of yourself!' He listened to her going slowly down the stairs.

'Ooh, Fred, it's cold!'

'Of course it's cold. Can you manage?'

'Yes. Ooooh!'

Twenty minutes later she re-emerged holding a tray. On it were a pot of tea, cups, plates, slices of hot toast, butter, marmalade, and two boiled eggs in their egg-cups.

'You're the most prodigious woman, Bessy, who ever walked God's earth.' He took the tray from her and put it down on the bed.

'Sorry, Fred, but I can't find the salt anywhere. And no

91

sugar. The basin was lying on the window-sill. Can't think how it got there, but the sugar's all dissolved. I found the milk but we can't touch that; the sea's in it and it's all gone grey and queer.'

'I've never had such a good breakfast.'

'Good job we keep so many things on that shelf. The water hasn't reached it, so the bread's dry, the butter's dry, the marmalade's dry. I had a devil of a job, though, finding any plates and knives. You've never seen such a mess in your life!'

'What about the stove?'

'Water's been over it, but it's gone down now. Lit first match. The flame's a bit funny, but it's working all right. Now you tuck in while I get these wet things off.'

She went out to find a towel. Grandpa listened to her rummaging in the cupboard, singing softly to herself:

> 'O Sacred Spirit, who didst brood
> Upon the chaos dark and rude,
> Who bad'st its angry tumult cease
> And gavest light and life and peace.'

She's a sacred spirit, he thought, and he filled his mouth with boiled egg. He switched on the radio; breakfast was never the same without light music and news and weather forecasts. But it was all music, not even a news flash to give him the comfort of knowing the outside world was aware of their predicament.

'A funny thing down there, Fred. When I'd boiled the eggs I didn't know where to put the water.'

'Why?'

'Didn't seem much point in throwing it into the sink when the floor's swimming, so I just chucked it anywhere. The sink is full of mud anyway.'

'What of it?'

'Well ... just seems wrong, somehow, pouring boiled

egg water on the floor. Not that I could see what was the floor and what was water. But I don't like doing that sort of thing, really.'

'Oh, Bessy!' Grandpa roared with laughter. She sipped her tea, and looked at him, wondering what the joke was.

Martin pulled himself up the stairs. Kathleen and the baby were asleep in Lynwyn's bed, Lynwyn was in his and beside her, he realized with a surge of joy, Aaron. Ann was dozing in a chair beside the fire. She opened her eyes.

'Martin! Oh, Martin!'

'Help me off with this suit. My hands won't work any more.' She peeled it off, and dried him with a towel. 'Peter's all right. He's asleep in bed. How did Ron get here?'

'I don't know. He collapsed just after he arrived. He's very ill; he ought to be in hospital. But all he could say was John is drowned.'

'John Hewitt drowned! Were they on the train? How did Ron escape?' He sat on the floor and put out his hands to the fire. 'I feel dizzy and weak.'

'Get into bed. I'll make you a hot drink.'

'Which bed? Lynwyn would be nice.'

'Would she?' said Lynwyn, who had woken up. She threw back the blanket and put on her dressing-gown. 'You lie there beside your brother and warm up. I'll see to the fire.'

Martin did so, but despite the heat of the bed, he was still shivering. He took the tea Ann held out to him, but he could not keep the cup still. She fed it to him, as if he were a baby. When he had finished she put the cup down, and stroked his face and hair.

'I do love you so much, Martin. I've been so thoughtless and selfish.'

'You have not.'

She kissed him, and lay against him on top of the bed-clothes, and soon he was asleep.

Later he woke with a dry mouth and a splitting headache. Feeling was restored to all his limbs, and every bone and muscle in him seemed to ache. The fire was dying and the candles had burned out. Ann was not in the room. He could hear her downstairs talking to Lynwyn. Aaron seemed to be awake; at least Martin could sense his body moving rest-lessly. After a while he realized that his brother was crying: there was no sound, but the movement was that of someone trying hard to control his tears.

'Ron.'

'Who's that? Where am I?'

'In Ann's flat. In bed. It's me, Martin.'

Aaron buried his face in the pillow. 'John Hewitt is drowned,' he said at last, trying to steady his voice. 'I tried to save him. I tried and tried.'

'Ron, it's all right.' Martin put his arms round his brother and pulled him closer.

'He was my friend.' Now the tears came more freely, warm and salt on Martin's face and throat. 'I do feel ill,' Aaron said at last, with a great sigh. 'My feet and hands are burning. So is my face. I feel sick and I can't be sick. My lungs are full, as if they want to burst.'

'Ann says you should be in hospital. We'll get you there as soon as we can.'

'Oh, I don't care. I wish I'd gone with John.'

'No you do not. Did you know that before I got into bed Lynwyn was sleeping here?'

'Was she?'

'There you were sharing a bed with a beautiful girl and you didn't even know it.'

'Just my luck.'

'That's better. That's not dying talk.'

Ann and Lynwyn came in. 'We've made baked beans on toast!' said Ann triumphantly. 'Lyn's camping stove is a marvel. Would you like some?'

'No thanks,' said Martin. 'Look, is there any milk? Heat some up for Ron, and give him some aspirins.'

'I don't want it,' said Aaron.

'You just shut up and do what you're told.'

'We must get a message to the hospital,' said Lynwyn, holding a candle close to Aaron's face. 'He looks dreadful. They must come out and take him.' She and Aaron stared at each other.

'What's going on outside?' Martin asked.

'The water hasn't gone down much,' said Ann. 'Two men rowed past in a dinghy a little while back. You can still hear people calling for help. There's traffic at times, grinding in low gear, swishing through water. Your car must be saturated. I don't somehow think you'll be going to college.'

'No, I don't suppose I will. What are we going to do? I mean where are Mum and Dad? The police want to evacuate Flatsea in the morning. Where will they go? David's? And what about us? If the water level doesn't fall I think we shall have to move out too.'

'We'll know soon. It's nearly morning.'

Lynwyn came up with the hot milk. Aaron took it without objection. Soon both brothers were asleep again. Ann and Lynwyn sat in front of the fire and talked.

Just before six o'clock Doris and Charley were ferried across Balaclava Street in a dinghy paddled by a helpful man from the Yacht Club. He could not negotiate the fallen tree, and Charley waded in up to his chest, Doris sitting on his shoulders. Upstairs they saw Aaron's blond hair and Martin's black hair on the pillows.

'Two of my babies,' whispered Doris. 'Fast asleep. Bless 'em.' She kissed both heads.

Ann recounted the night's adventures, and assured them that Peter was safe.

'It seems as if David's the only one of the family not involved,' she said. 'I suppose he's safe and sound in bed, not a care in the world.'

'He's had just as bad a shock as any of us,' Charley said.

'The sea can't have reached there! That's impossible.'

'Oh, he's kept his feet dry, I grant you. But Peter phoned him when the water was just coming into the pub. That put him in a state, I can tell you. He's spent half the night driving round Oozedam, trying to get news of us all. The police told him about the hospital. No one's hurt there, but it was completely cut off. Poor David! He's in more of a state than when Kevin was born, worried out of his mind about Pat and the baby. We found him at his house, pacing up and down, smoking cigarette after cigarette.'

'And is Pat all right?'

'Sure to be. She's on the fourth floor. There can't be any heat or light, but babies are tough.'

'You men!' Doris said. 'You don't know anything!'

'Little Donna's been right in the water,' said Ann. 'And she seems none the worse for it.'

Later Lynwyn came in with the ambulance men and they took Aaron out on a stretcher. He did not wake.

'Looks like frostbite,' said one of the men.

'I must put on some dry clothes,' said Lynwyn, and went downstairs. Ann followed her.

'You like him, don't you?'

'Who?'

'Ron.'

Lynwyn hesitated, then said, 'A bit.' They smiled at each other. 'Look, I must get to work somehow. There's probably a great mess of rubbish to clear at the shop. Do you think Ron's Dad would carry me out into Pretoria Street? If I leave it much longer the water will make it impossible. Are you going to work?'

'No. You're pretty keen, leaving for work at this hour of the morning!'

'I'm wide awake. Might as well get on with it.'

'I'm dead tired. When those two have gone I'm going to crawl in beside Martin and sleep the clock round.'

Grandpa listened to the news at eight o'clock. Severe gales had brought havoc to Scotland, causing a number of shipping disasters in the North Sea. An enormous number of trees had been uprooted, and the roofs of several houses in Aberdeen and Edinburgh had been blown off. The floods were too recent for detailed news: 'Reports are coming in of widespread flooding after last night's high tide along the whole length of the East Coast from the Humber to Margate. There has been considerable structural damage to many seaside properties and it is feared that a number of people may have lost their lives. It is too early yet to estimate either the extent of the damage or the number of missing persons.' The weather forecast that followed said that the 'vigorous trough of low pressure' which had produced the high wind was now moving eastwards. Gales would die down everywhere, but it would be cold, with the possibility of isolated showers of snow or sleet.

'It is cold,' Grandpa said. Bessy was still asleep, her face flushed; probably a high temperature, he thought, after her efforts in the small hours with breakfast. He dressed and went downstairs. The water had drained out of the house, leaving the rooms almost unrecognizable. The lino, slippery with inches of black mud, squelched underfoot. The furniture was all wrecked, the chairs a heap of matchwood and the table lying on its side. Broken china and glass were strewn everywhere, all those precious family relics, some of them saved and loved for over a century. Saddest of all to Grandpa was the embroidered sampler that had hung all his life over the fireplace; a picture of a house surrounded by the alphabet in capital letters, sewn by his great-grandmother, with her name and the date, *Rachel Cross 1831*. It was lying upside down in the grate, its glass shattered, the material sodden and torn.

He put on his gumboots and went outside. The chickenhouse had been too well-made, the wood firmly secured in a concrete base, and the water had not smashed it. If it had floated free the birds might have had a chance, but every one of them was dead. Most of the plants in his little garden looked as if they had been trampled to pieces; and the lawn was covered with dead worms, whitened by the sea. Clouds of screeching gulls overhead flapped and swooped, enjoying this unexpected feast.

He went out into the road. This, too, was covered in thick oozy mud and he found it difficult to keep his balance. The haystack opposite, which belonged to the farmer, Alf Brookfield, had disappeared. A few wisps of straw showed that it had existed. Telephone wires and electricity cables sagged or were snapped off, and where they hung down low seaweed and twigs festooned them. His neighbours were busy clearing up. Women mopped their floors. Their menfolk carried out furniture and soaked carpets, in the hope that the sun would dry them before the next high tide came up and forced them to carry everything inside again. Alf

Brookfield's parrot, which must have escaped from its cage in the night, sat on a branch of a tree, watching.

Grandpa walked towards the sea. The fields were ruined, covered in places by mud, the grass battered and flattened. The salt would poison the earth for years to come. There were many dead animals, pigs and cows, some of them caught in the barbed wire fences as they had tried to flee the engulfing water; and the countryside was littered with debris – plastic containers, dustbins, wood. Even a boat, seemingly intact, perched on top of a hedge. He could not reach the sea wall for there was still too much water caught behind it. But he could see at least one gaping hole several yards in length where it had been crumbled to ground level, leaving a great jumble of boulders and layers of mud and sand spread over the grass. The tide was beginning to flow in again over the land. The wall would take days to repair, and dozens of men : they would be flooded out many times yet before the sea was safely where it should be. He stared out across the estuary, to Oozedam, and even to his old eyes things seemed different. The town itself, at this distance, looked normal, but elsewhere great sheets of water covered acres of the land. The sea was not the fury and force it had been last night, but it was grey, rough, and restless, a stiff breeze tossing its surface into white ridges.

His footsteps led him, by force of habit more than conscious thought, in the direction of The King's Head. Outside the pub were four landrovers. A police car came slowly along the road towards him relaying over its loudspeaker a message which was repeated several times. 'This is the police. The island must be evacuated before high tide. Please bring only essential possessions with you. Everything else that is movable should be placed upstairs. When you are ready report to the army transport at The King's Head.'

Peter, white-faced with anger, was arguing furiously with a policeman, who stepped back to avoid being splashed with dirty water from the mop the boy was brandishing.

'Grandpa!' he shouted. 'They say we've got to leave! I won't!'

'You haven't got any choice.'

'Are you related to this lad?' the policeman asked. 'Just make him see reason, will you? If they're all as stubborn as this one, we'll end up marooned here before we can move anyone out.' He walked off in the direction of the next house.

'What do you think you're trying to do?' Grandpa asked.

'Clean the place out before opening time.' He looked inside and Grandpa followed the direction of his gaze. Susan was on her hands and knees with a pail of hot water and a scrubbing-brush, cleaning the floor.

'Peter ... You've some spirit, I'll say that. But it's no use. The sea'll be right up here again soon.'

'I've got sandbags filled. We'll keep it out. I've been working for hours.' Grandpa shook his head sadly. Peter went back indoors, shouting, 'I'm not going unless Dad tells me to.'

Grandpa followed him. 'Your Dad's not here, so you'd better listen to me for once.'

Peter looked down at his feet, then back at his grandfather, and said, quietly, 'No.'

Grandpa sighed. 'If you really wanted to help your Dad you'd stop messing about with scrubbing floors and filling sandbags, and you'd start putting the stock upstairs. Get all that sherry and spirits and tonics into a bedroom and lock 'em in a cupboard. And the beer out of the cellar, that should go up too. And stop being such a headstrong young fool!!'

And he walked out before his grandson could reply. On the way back to his cottage, he met another policeman. 'Are you going to seal off the island?' he asked.

'We're putting a road-block on the bridge. You'll be allowed back on certain days to clean up, but we can't risk anybody staying here at night. And don't worry, we shan't let anyone near to do any looting.'

'There's not much left worth stealing.'

'You'll be away for at least three weeks. So take what you need.'

Everything downstairs in the cottage could be left as it was. But he picked up the old sampler and removed the splinters of glass, then rinsed it out under the kitchen tap and squeezed it dry. That he would take. If it wasn't completely spoiled he'd give it to Peter.

The sea was rushing in over the island when the evacuation began. Susan had gone when her parents called for her, but Peter had to be forcibly dragged out by two policemen, and was thrown unceremoniously onto the floor of a landrover. He said nothing during the journey, but seethed in silent indignation. His parents had arrived soon after eight, and together they had moved most of the stock upstairs, but there were still kegs of beer left in the cellar. Charley told him to leave them. Peter had not left in the car as Doris had filled it with luggage the family needed, clothes mostly, but also Aaron's guitar, which Peter thought was not an essential possession. When they left he had returned to the cellar, and there the police found him.

Few of the people in the army transport had much to say. Most of the islanders had coped well with the catastrophe of the flood; after the initial shock and horror they had kept themselves alive and cheerful. Nobody had been drowned. Some were justifiably proud of their endurance, or deeds they had performed during the night; now this forcible ejection from their land and property was a second appalling blow, however necessary it might appear to the authorities, which humiliated them in a way the sea had failed to do. When the landrovers arrived at Peter's school it was a very despondent and bewildered crowd of people who climbed out.

Part Three
Afterwards

When Martin woke and looked at his watch he was surprised to see that it was past mid-day. Ann was asleep beside him. Aaron, he supposed, had been taken to hospital, but he was puzzled that this had happened without his being woken by the noise or movement. There was no sign of Lynwyn, or Kathleen and her baby. He put on his clothes and went to the window. The tide had come up again while he slept, but now it was falling. It was like Venice. A West Indian family a few doors down on the other side of the street was being taken out through a first-floor window. They were all in their best clothes, bright and multi-coloured. A frail rocking boat was lashed between two window-frames and the people were being lowered slowly and with great difficulty. Two little girls, their frizzy hair in white ribbons, sat close together on a thwart, their faces solemn and a little frightened, but there were shouts and laughter from the adults.

Their neighbours watched, waving and giving advice. The old man next door to them looked down in silence, smoking a pipe. Many of the windows were empty, and Martin guessed that these were houses that had already been evacuated. A punt passed, low in the water and laden with staring people, who looked as if in other circumstances they would have been sight-seers. Canoes paddled by in both directions, and a dinghy, empty except for its steersman, moved towards another waiting family.

Another boat came close, carefully avoiding the roof of

his car, which was a dark rippling shape just below the surface. One of the men in it was throwing food in to the stranded people. Martin decided he was hungry, and went down to Lynwyn's room in order to get closer. He pushed up the window.

'What do you want, mate? Sausages, cigarettes, coffee, sandwiches.'

'I'm starving. Anything you can spare.'

He leaned right out, and the man passed him up a hot dog, a cheese sandwich, a plastic mug of coffee, and two cigarettes.

'How many in there?'

'Two of us.'

'All right, are you? No casualties?'

'No, we're fine.'

'Shouldn't be long before the boats get to you.' He paddled on.

Martin ate and drank, leaving the sandwich and a cigarette for Ann. He lit his, and stared out at the scene. The water was filthy, and filled with an enormous quantity of rubbish, children's toys, balls, orange-peel, cabbages, a dead cat, seaweed, plants, paper. A thin film of petrol, red, blue and purple, made beautiful constantly changing patterns on the surface. A boy leaned out of the window directly opposite, fishing with a home-made rod. He grinned at Martin and waved. 'A great day for the fish!' he shouted.

'Caught anything?'

'Three shoes! How's your mate?'

'What mate?'

'The one they took out on the stretcher.'

'My brother. I don't know.'

'They had to move that tree first. Did you see them?'

'I was asleep.'

'A crane moved it. Made a mess of that car outside your house.'

'Did it indeed!'

He threw his cigarette end into the water, shut the window, and went upstairs. Ann was still asleep, so he went into the bathroom, and looked out at the scene at the back of the house. It was much more desolate. There were no people; just water, grey and dirty, stretching back to the railway line, lapping at Kathleen's windows, covering the gardens, breaking over the tops of fences and washing-line posts. A garden shed which had somehow remained airtight was drifting slowly with the wind a few doors away, a cat placidly sitting on its roof, washing its face. The road, away to his right, curved slightly, so the backs of the houses further down were more clearly visible than those of his near neighbours. Some of them had been badly damaged: curtains flapped out of broken windows; the whole rear wall of the two end houses had completely collapsed and what was left was like a bombed ruin, the inhabitants' wallpaper, fireplaces, tables, chairs and beds open to anyone who cared to look.

Much of the ballast and a large quantity of earth from the top of the railway embankment had been washed away, and the lines, still intact, hung in places in mid-air. The allotments beyond were under several feet of water and jagged pieces of concrete stuck out, slabs of the breached wall that had been hurled forwards by the inrush of the sea. Here several more sheds floated, and dead animals, mostly pigs. There were also a large number of unusually-shaped boxes which Martin guessed were coffins; there was an undertaker's yard next to the railway bridge. From his left, on the other side of the houses, came the sound of a police loudspeaker, broadcasting several warnings and pleas for help.

He suddenly felt very depressed. Last night there had been the hardships of the freezing cold water, the journey to Flatsea – that now seemed a curiously dream-like episode in the night's events – ; there had been moments too of sheer terror, but there had also been excitement, relief, a sense of doing something of desperate importance. Now the disruption of normality was dreary and pointless. It might be days before ordinary life could begin again. He returned to the living-room, and began to look through the pile of his pictures stacked against the wall. They were mostly pencil sketches or pen-and-ink drawings, but some were oils on canvas or sugar-paper. A few were framed. There were scenes of Flatsea, one of Balaclava Street, a sketch of Aaron done a long time ago; but most of them were of Ann or Ann and himself in different places in this room. It was an obsessive theme, this, their private world; Ann reading in front of the fire, or lying in bed, or in the bath, then just her face (several times), or her face and his, the two of them looking out of the window, a copy of Picasso's *La Vie* with himself and Ann as the man and woman embracing protectively, the two of them cooking at the stove, himself shaving, himself idle and bored. This was all that mattered, this girl, this room.

'Martin.' She had woken up. 'It wasn't a nightmare?'

'It really happened. And I came back.'

'So you did.' She smiled and held her arms out to him. 'Come and kiss me.' He knelt beside her. 'How warm you are now! And I was afraid, terrified you would die. Martin, I behaved very selfishly.'

'You did not.'

'I did. You know I did. You said so. And I'm sorry. You've seen a bad side of me.'

'I've known you for years and years.'

'Not as bad as that. I don't know why. I don't know.'

'You were just frightened.'

'Yes, but it's no excuse. I'm glad in a way you had to make that pointless journey to Peter. I was left on my own ... I know Kathleen and Lynwyn were here, and Ron came ... but I hadn't got you, and I thought I might never see you again. You could have been drowned. I can't describe it. It was so ... desolate.'

'I'm here now.'

'Yes. Never go away again, never.'

'Last night won't happen again. Nothing quite like that, anyway.'

'I do want to marry you, Martin ... that's what those hours meant. Now. Tomorrow, or the soonest we can. Say something.'

'I don't know what. Now you've said it I can't believe it. Say it again.'

'No. You say yes.'

'Yes.'

'I do love you.'

He was silent a long time, not knowing how to put the flood of delight in his body into words. When the words came they were so prosaic. 'At the registry office you buy a licence, don't you? How soon after that can you marry?'

'One whole day.'

'Let's go there now.'

'I should go and see him anyway. He's my boss after all. The office will be a floating mass of papers.'

'All those certificates going back all those years lost.'

'To 1837. They're in books, and locked away in safes, so they're probably quite dry.'

'I shall ask Ron to be my best man.'

'But he's in hospital.'

'Can we wait till he comes out?'

'Yes. Lynwyn can be bridesmaid.'

'Let's go now. And then find my parents and tell them.'

'Later.'

'How long is it we've known each other?'

'Ever since I can remember.'

'I used to think you were ugly.'

'So were you when you were about thirteen. Thin and spotty.'

'I love you.'

'Come back to bed, Martin.'

'Yes.' He kissed her eyes and lips and shoulders. 'You are beautiful.'

'So are you. So are you.'

Aaron was full of grumbles at being kept in hospital. After his long sleep and a good meal he felt almost normal, physically, apart from a mild ache in his lungs and a hot itchy sensation in his feet and hands. He was told that the irritation was due to frostbite, but he could not see why this should keep him in bed. The treatment was unpleasant. He had to put his hands and feet in what seemed like unbearably hot water, and he was not reassured by the nurse telling him that the water was in fact almost cold.

He was an unco-operative patient. Eventually the nurse said with exasperation 'Don't you realize what can happen if you neglect frostbite?'

'Nothing much I should imagine.'

'It can lead to gangrene.'

'Gangrene!'

'And you know what that means. We have to amputate.'

'Amputate!!'

'Yes. Don't keep repeating everything I say. Chop chop chop!'

He was surprised to see Lynwyn come hesitantly down the ward and stop by his bed.

'The sister agreed it was all right,' she said, when the nurse looked at her questioningly.

'To see this young man? Perhaps you can drill some sense into him. Are you his girlfriend?'

'Er —'

'Well, just see he keeps taking his feet in and out of that bowl.' She went away to another patient. Aaron smirked and Lynwyn looked embarrassed.

'Perhaps I shouldn't have come,' she said.

'Why?'

'I wanted to know how you were. You were very ill. Sick everywhere and delirious. I went for the ambulance. Now put your feet back in that water!'

'It's too bloody hot.'

'Do as I said or I'll fetch the nurse!'

He glared at her, then smiled, and put his feet back for as long as he could bear it.

'How did you manage outside? The ground's flooded out.'

'They're busy pumping it away. It's nearly all gone. Look, I've brought you some things. There's not many shops open ... so it's fruit and magazines I had in the flat.'

She was attractive. This was interesting. 'Can you show me? My hands.' He held them out to her. The fingers were swollen and bent only with difficulty. 'They're frozen, I suppose. I don't think I can turn the pages.'

'They're pop magazines. I've seen you playing at the Moulin Rouge Club. You're good.' The nurse was coming back down the ward. Martin and Ann were standing at the door. 'I think I'd better go now. It's not visiting hours.'

'Will you come again?'

She hesitated. 'If you want me to, yes.'

'I do. When I get out of here will you come out with me?'

She laughed. 'You don't waste much time, do you?'

'Please.'

'Yes. I'd like to.'

'It's all very irregular,' said the nurse, taking Aaron's feet out of the bowl. 'I don't know how this girl got in here at all.' Lynwyn winked and hurried away. 'Your brother is here with his fiancée and says he must see you very urgently. But only for five minutes. Put your hands in this bowl.'

Fiancée? What did it mean? Martin and Ann were standing by his bed, arms round each other, grinning happily. They said nothing, waiting for the nurse to go, but she stayed, holding Aaron's hands in the water.

'Don't tell me,' he said. 'I've guessed. You're getting married.'

'On Thursday,' said Martin, 'at the registry office. Ron, I want you to be my best man.'

'Do you really?'

'Why not? You *are* my best man.'

Aaron smiled. 'Did you see Lynwyn?' he asked.

'I must get some more water,' said the nurse. 'It should be a little warmer.'

'I think she likes you,' said Ann.

'Does she?'

'Though she's six years older than you.'

They were silent. Martin fidgeted.

'Have they found his body?' Aaron asked.

'Yes.'

'When is the funeral?'

'I'm not sure. 'There's to be an inquest on all the people who were drowned. I suppose the funerals will be after that.'

'Martin ... will you ask Mum and Dad to buy a wreath, and send a card. Ron, with all my love?' He screwed up his face, and hid in the pillow. 'Go away, Martin.' Martin touched his brother's arm, but Aaron pushed his hand off. 'You only make it worse!'

'Martin,' said Ann. 'Leave him.'

When they had gone the nurse came back with another bowl of water and plunged Aaron's hands in it. 'What's the matter?' she asked. 'Did they upset you?'

'No. It's nothing. My God, that's hot!'

'Just be brave. If it's all going well, you can be out the day after tomorrow.'

The treatment continued for another half hour, then the nurse dried his hands. She stroked his fingers, softly and smoothly, bending the joints, then did the same with his toes. 'Does it tickle?' she asked.

'Yes. There's a sort of sensation there. Erotic.'

'Don't be absurd.' She bent his toes backwards and forwards more vigorously. 'What about that?'

'It hurts!'

'Good. You'll be all right quite soon.' She smiled cheerfully. 'When people have frostbitten toes they sometimes fall off. Not very nice, is it?'

'No.'

'I'm going to bandage your hands and feet. Then I want you to sleep.'

'I don't feel a bit sleepy.'

'I'm going to give you a tablet.' He made a face at her.

'Now these bandages will cover your hands and feet completely. You won't be able to use your fingers at all until I take them off. Cheer up, worse things happen at sea.'

The pill made him drowsy very quickly. As he fell asleep the shape of the pillow and the gentle breathing movement of his chest against the sheets became the movement of the sea, and he was back in the icy water fighting for John's life. There were his staring drowned eyes: somehow Aaron knew that the seeing was gone, even while he was pushing breath back into the useless lungs. He forced the picture out of his head. Lynwyn. Would she be any different from all the girls he had known? He hoped so. It was time now to begin his life properly.

Martin and Ann, after leaving Aaron, went upstairs to the maternity ward. Pat was well, though very tired; baby Kevin was asleep in a crib beside her, only his little face visible.

'Of course he looks like David!' Martin said. 'What nonsense Mum talks!'

'What a night it's been here!' Pat said. 'No light, no heat, and no one's had a wink of sleep. Kevin's certainly had a dramatic start to things.'

'We're getting married,' Martin said. 'On Thursday.'

'Oh, I'm so glad! Martin, give me a hug.' He did so, feeling guilty about the rude remarks they sometimes made about Pat being plain, her not fitting in to his family's way of life. She was a warm friendly person, an ideal wife for David. He kissed her with real affection.

'Here!' said Ann. 'He's marrying me!'

Martin laughed. 'Have you seen Ron?' he asked Pat.

'Yes.' Her face clouded. 'Bad. He's quite shattered. About John, I mean. I didn't know they were so close.'

'I don't think Ron knew himself.'

'You two! Out!' A nurse bore down on them. 'How did you get in here? We've quite enough trouble without visitors adding to it.'

'See you,' Pat said. 'Look after each other.'

Charley and Doris picked Peter up at the school. They were all going to stay at David's until they were allowed back home. However, his little house had only two bedrooms and when Aaron joined them it would be bursting at the seams. Peter would have to sleep on the sofa then; it was felt that the hospital patient was more in need of a proper rest than the stalwart defender of The King's Head. 'But at least,' Doris said, 'David will get good meals now, what with Pat being away.' There was much heart-searching as to what to do with Grandpa and Grandma. They could not go to Aunt Sal's in Tilbury, for like them she had been flooded out. There was just not enough room for them at David's, and though they knew dozens of people in Oozedam and the surrounding area, no one could take them in. Most of their friends had been washed out of their homes too.

They were to be billeted in a disused army camp with three hundred others. It was about five miles away from David's house. Doris said, trying to be cheerful, that that wasn't far; Charley would come every day and drive them to the hospital to see the new baby, or wherever they wanted. But the old people were miserable. On the island Grandpa lived only a few doors away from his son; though Charley had been away during his National Service just after the war, he had otherwise never been further off since then, except for holidays.

'I shan't get used to it,' Grandpa said, looking glum. He

was sitting on his suitcase in the middle of the school hall.

'Neither shall I,' said Bessy. 'Do you think them places are clean, Charley?'

'What places?'

'This here camp. I don't suppose soldiers know much about keeping a place clean.'

'There's no soldiers there now,' said Charley patiently. 'It's the W.V.S. will be looking after you.'

'Never happened to us, never, not even in '97,' said Grandpa. 'Not even in Hitler's war. Where's the nearest pub, Charley; can you tell me that?'

'Er ... the Dog and Fox, I think, at the Maldon turning.'

'That's about a mile off! How can I do that?'

'I'll take you in the car.'

'Not the same as a good walk down to The King's Head.'

'The beer will be just as good.'

'It won't.'

Nothing that could be said was of the slightest consolation. Charley suggested that he and Doris went to the army camp, and Grandma and Grandpa went to David's. Doris looked amazed, but tactfully said nothing.

'Wouldn't hear of it,' said Grandma. 'The idea! Don't think because we're old we can't manage. We'll be all right, don't you worry. Haven't lived this long to let a little thing like this upset me.'

'Be a bit of a strain on you, Bess. Cooking for five.'

'Oh, I can cook, Fred. Why, when I was in service –'

'That was sixty-five years ago.'

'Don't think I couldn't do it, because I could. No. I'll go where they put me.' But when it was time for them to go – they had to travel in special coaches rather than private cars; it made the administration easier – Grandma was crying.

*

The next few days were busy. When the tide was low the inhabitants of Flatsea were allowed back on the island to clean out their houses and tidy up. They had to obtain a special pass from the police, which stated that they were bona fide residents, and this had to be shown to the constable on duty at the bridge. Grandma hated this idea; she had lived on Flatsea for more than fifty years and now she was required to prove it. So she refused to come; she stayed in the camp and sulked, but when Doris and Charley visited the hospital on the Tuesday she did go with them. She was delighted with her first great-grandson. But the news that Martin and Ann were to be married did not please her. She said that a registry office wedding was not a proper marriage, and she would not be seen dead in such a place. Doris, however, was relieved and thrilled, and made Charley drive her to Ipswich on Wednesday to buy new clothes. Charley decided to give a party for the bride and groom. It would be held in The King's Head as soon as they were allowed back there permanently, and with any luck it would coincide with Aaron's eighteenth birthday.

The school had a week's holiday. Though the number of homeless dropped after the first day there were still plenty of strangers wandering around the building, and too many children were shocked or bewildered by the events of Sunday night for lessons to be resumed with any hope of normal work being done. Several others were away ill after their soaking; some had lost parents or brothers and sisters.

Monday evening and all day Tuesday saw an influx of pressmen and television crews into Oozedam. Peter and Susan, who had gone up to the school to meet some of the pupils in their class, told their story to the cameras. They were bitterly disappointed that they could see nothing of this on the television, for the town was still without electricity. The papers on Tuesday morning contained the first detailed news of the disaster, and Oozedam people found that their town was just a small part of a much larger pattern; along whole stretches of the coasts of Lincolnshire, Norfolk, Suffolk, Essex and Kent, the sea, prevented from ebbing on Sunday by the ferocity of the wind, had surged inwards and smashed down sea-defences as if they were children's toys. About three hundred people, it was estimated, had been drowned, and every port or fishing village or seaside holiday town had a dramatic story to tell. In Oozedam thirty-five people had lost their lives, ten of them in the first coach of the wrecked train. The stories about Oozedam centred on both this and the collapse of the sea wall that had put the power station out of action, raining pieces of concrete onto it like bombs.

Peter was in love. He knew Susan felt the same. But neither of them could say so; they were too shy. He slept badly and ate little, and looked at himself in the mirror wondering if his eyes gave his secret away. There was a lightness in his body that was extraordinary : he almost felt no longer part of gravity. He was glad Aaron was not at home. His brother would know the signs and make cynical comments. Mum and Dad were (Peter thought) too old to remember.

Susan and her parents were staying with her mother's sister, about a mile from David's house. When the families went to Flatsea, Peter and Susan went with them, and walked about the island, and the grey level landscape seemed enchanted. Sometimes they went into Oozedam and watched the town's efforts to rid itself of the sea. They stared at the huge pumping-machines expelling the water from the area near the hospital and the power station, and the cranes and earth-removers piling boulders, clay and sand into the innumerable breaches in the walls. It was the most marvellous week of his life.

One evening they quarrelled. Peter was hurt when she said his desire to take over his father's pub was unambitious. One remark led to another, and eventually she ran home, refusing to let him come with her. He sat alone on the edge of a chair, listening to the silence. Was it all finished? He tried to read, but could not see the print. He went out and walked down to her house, wondering if he had enough courage to knock and see her, but he did not dare face her parents; they would know there had been an argument. He stood in the trees on the other side of the road and looked at the house, wishing he had put on a sweater and a coat. As he grew colder, he was reminded more and more of Sunday night and the petrifying chill of that black flood, the start of their happiness. The lights downstairs glimmered red, warm and inviting; they flickered, dulled and brightened, for the town was now using an emergency generator, and was not on full power. Then her bedroom light was switched on; she looked out and his heart turned over. He was sure that she had seen him. The curtains shut with one angry sweep.

But she came to David's early next morning and apologized. 'Why were you standing under the trees?'

'I don't know.' He blushed and fiddled about with the newspaper.

'It frightened me.'

'I thought it was all over.'

'You're too . . . intense, Peter.'

'It was silly. Nothing.'

'It's not all over, is it?'

'Of course not.' He smiled. Their heads were close, huge, out of focus; her face was soft and loving; he could see every pore of her skin and every fine hair, and he longed to be that face, in it, part of it. He put his hands on her cheeks and said 'I love you.'

When Martin and Ann returned from the hospital on Monday it was dark, and there was no boat to ferry them across to the house. So once again they became soaking wet up to their waists. It was the last straw. As they dried themselves Martin wondered whether they should move out altogether for the time being. They were without gas and electricity and it was freezing cold: the front door was still wedged inside the hall; the windows in Kathleen's flat were broken, and the back door was so swollen it would not shut. The ground floor was completely uninhabitable. Kathleen and her baby had left while Martin and Ann slept; she had gone to stay with some Irish friends on the other side of town.

Martin thought he should return to Ipswich. He had missed a day at college, and he felt there was no good reason for staying away any longer. His car was a wreck. He decided to thumb a lift, and come back on Wednesday night, as the wedding was to be at mid-day on Thursday. Ann refused to go with him. She had to work in the morning; the registrar could not be expected to clean out the office on his own. When they had called there earlier, he was trying to cope by candlelight with mopping up and sweeping out debris. It would be days before the place was fit to be used again. It was only because Ann was an employee that he agreed to marry them on Thursday.

Ann said she would stay in the flat. Martin told her she would freeze or starve. In the middle of the argument Lynwyn arrived to say that she was packing, and Ann eventually agreed to go with her. There was a room over the shoe-shop where she worked that was used as a store; they could both camp down there for a night or two.

'And if you're ready in half an hour,' said Lynwyn, 'there's a boat coming to pick me up. The man who brought me across after I left the hospital said he'd come back for me.'

'One thing we haven't thought of, Martin,' said Ann. 'During the week I work here and you're in Ipswich. Are we going on like that, with you coming home Friday evening till Monday morning?'

'We could move.'

'We could. Else it's another five terms.'

'Come and live with me and be my love in Ipswich.'

'And lose this flat. You wouldn't want to, Martin.'

'How unromantic you are,' said Lynwyn. 'I've never met a couple like it. I think this house is horrible, but I can't afford anything better.'

'You don't have to be romantic.'

'No.' Lynwyn sighed. 'I can see that. Yet you are so obviously lovers. I just can't understand it.'

'Mutual need.'

'So that's all it is,' said Ann.

'Maybe there's more to it.'

'Go and pack,' said Lynwyn, laughing.

Grandpa was looking forward to the wedding, but Bessy grumbled about it so much that he decided he dared not go.

'We never thought about registry offices,' she said. 'It's not right. Weddings should be in church.'

Grandpa yawned. 'If you say so, Bessy.'

'Church was good enough for us. Should be good enough for them.'

'People think different.'

'Not my favourite grandson, Martin. Never was. Artist!' She sniffed disapprovingly.

'He's a good boy. One of the best. Saved a girl and a baby from drowning on Sunday, didn't he?'

'Doesn't excuse living together like that with Ann.'

'Oh, give over, Bess.'

'All this rush,' Grandma went on relentlessly. 'What's the rush for? That's what I'd like to know.'

'Rush? Why, they've been going out together for five years or more. They've known each other since they were kids. Young people's ways is just different from ours.'

'Darn sight worse than ours.'

'I'm going out.'

'That's right. Leave me in this dump all on my own, while you go off boozing. Just like you.'

'If I stop will you promise to keep quiet? I've heard just about all I can stand.'

Grandma was silent. The problem was simply that the army camp wasn't home. She was a great worker, devoted to sewing, cleaning, cooking, pottering in her garden, and she fretted when everything was done for her, particularly when it was done with the kindest of intentions. She intensely disliked accepting charity in any form, and the generosity of people to the flood victims really distressed her. Nation-wide appeals had been made for gifts of clothes, bedding and food, and Oozedam was, like other places, inundated by the response. Heaps of second-hand clothes were already piled in the camp store; the canteen had great difficulty in storing all the food parcels it was sent. Sweets and chocolate arrived in vast quantities, many with touching messages, and the inhabitants of the camp, Grandma thought, made pigs of themselves. There was only one way to vent her feelings, and that was on her relatives; Charley and Doris put up with it forbearingly, but Fred, who had to listen for much longer than they did, was aggravated to the limit of his endurance.

On Thursday she suddenly decided she would go into Oozedam with Charley and Doris, but not to the wedding. The inquest on the flood victims was to be opened that morning in the Town Hall, and she wanted to hear it. Her life-long friend, Nellie Meal, had been one of those who had died, not by drowning, but from shock and exposure soon after she had been evacuated from her bungalow. She was the old lady who had sat, unable to speak, in the police car which had given Martin a lift on his journey back from Flatsea.

'I want to hear what happened to her, Fred. It's the least we can do for her, going to listen.' Fred had to go with her.

Aaron was able to leave hospital on the Thursday morning. There was still some pain in his feet so that he had to walk slowly, and his fingers were bandaged. This spoiled his appearance at the wedding a little, Doris thought, though he looked quite handsome in his pearl grey suit; more than Martin, who had refused to buy any new clothes for the occasion, but wore instead his flowered shirt, blue trousers and his iron cross. She was rather annoyed with Lynwyn for stealing the limelight by appearing in a magnificent traditional West Indian dress. Ron, the stupid fool, could not take his eyes off her; he would ruin his piece with the ring if he did not pay more attention.

It was all over very quickly. Martin thought they would go to the nearest pub and have a few drinks, but his father had booked a table at the Clarence, the best hotel in town.

Afterwards, Lynwyn thought she should go back to the shop as she had not been given the afternoon off, and

Aaron went with her. Peter followed. He was meeting Susan outside the Odeon. The electricity had been restored that day, and on Ron's recommendation they were going to 'A Teenage Werewolf's Chick', the first performance of it that had been possible since Sunday night. David went to the hospital to see Pat, and, left with just Charley, Martin and Ann, and relaxed with the drink, Doris decided that she had always liked Ann, always hoped she and Martin would marry, that it was only this spending the weekends together that had bothered her and that was now over: Ann was one of the family. She said all this several times until Charley told her to stop.

Eventually Martin and Ann left. They wanted to see Pat and the baby before returning to Balaclava Street, where they hoped to spend the night. Charley ordered two more Drambuies.

'Funny sort of wedding altogether,' said Doris. 'Why couldn't she wear white?'

'Their wedding. It's what they wanted.'

'Can't help feeling let down, though. This Art College isn't doing Martin much good.'

'What do you mean?'

'Well ... Look at the way he was dressed!'

'No good us complaining.'

'I know that. Children aren't your possessions. They're just borrowed for a while.'

'So what's the matter?'

'I just wish ... well, that he'd compromise a bit. He was never any trouble, Martin, not like Ron. Now I don't seem to know him any more.'

'That's not so, Doris. If you had objected that strongly to the way he behaves you would have lost him. Martin! No.

He loves us just as much as he ever did. This long hair, wearing beads, all that sort of thing: that's not what comes to my mind when I think of Martin. I think of him going out on that surfboard to see if he could save his young brother from drowning.'

'It's all very well, Charley. You just don't see the problems. Take Ron, for instance. Gone all silly over that Lynwyn ... she's a nice girl, I can see that. Made a very good impression, despite that showy dress. But suppose they got serious?'

'What does it matter?'

'A lot. Suppose they got married. The difficulties. Half-caste children.'

'Married? Gracious, woman, what are you talking about? They haven't even been out together, not once! And him only seventeen! You do make mountains!'

'All the same, Ron does make life difficult for himself.'

'I think of him too on Sunday night. I talked to one of the men who was on that train. Said there was nothing Ron didn't do to try and save John. Complete disregard of his own safety.'

'You're forgetting one thing, Charley. If they'd all been a bit more responsible, none of this would have happened. If Ron had come home on the earlier train, John would still be alive. Martin should never have left the pub, and Peter shouldn't have persuaded them to go. If they'd all done what they were supposed to do, they'd have been safe upstairs. Probably never got a foot wet.'

'Well ... you can't expect them to have our judgement. Think they know best, and find out the hard way.'

'So hard there's a young lad drowned. That's what I see.'

'You can't blame Ron for that. He didn't make John miss the train. John had to make his own decisions.'

'Yes. And he's dead.'

'Peter, too. Don't forget him. Rescued Susan, went up to see if Mum and Dad were all right, started cleaning down the pub.'

'He's besotted with that girl.'

'Just remember when you were nearly sixteen. Natural thing to happen.'

'He's so serious, Peter. He'd be broken up if it all finished.'

'Probably break it up himself. At that age these things stop as suddenly as they start.'

'I remember breaking off our engagement twice, Charley. Seems very idiotic now.'

'I thought so at the time. But I'm sorry I've lost that ring. I just took it off to wash my hands, like I always do. Now Lord knows where the sea's carried it.'

'You're as thoughtless as your sons.'

'Come off it, Doris. If you really felt as bad as you talk, our kids would have cleared off years ago, or be waiting their first chance to do so.'

'I know damn well you can't interfere once they're a certain age. It's not easy, though.'

'There you are ... we think exactly the same, then.'

'Must be something wrong if that's true.'

'They're good kids, I know that. I do love 'em!'

'So do I!'

When Martin and Ann returned to Balaclava Street they found the Council had been there and put the front door back on its hinges. Pinned on it was a notice:

'I'm not going to start married life in a refugee camp,'
said Ann.

'Then come to Ipswich with me.'

'What about my job?'

'I've had enough of this. Come on, back to the registrar.'

'What for?'

'Because he's going to give you tomorrow off. And all
next week, if necessary, until we can move back. And don't
argue.'

Which the registrar agreed, with some reluctance, to
allow. They went to the shoe-shop to tell Lynwyn. Aaron
was still there, pretending to be a customer, and he agreed to
pass the message on to the rest of the family.

So, in the gathering dusk Martin and Ann, with a few
possessions in a rucksack, began their marriage walking up
the Ipswich road, thumbing a lift.

Friday, Saturday and Sunday were mild days; Doris and
Charley were able to spend a great deal of time on the island,
Peter and Susan helping. Susan's parents were busy cleaning
out their house, too, and though she gave them a hand at
first, they knew where she would prefer to be, and sent
her off to The King's Head.

Restoring the pub to a state of normality was going to
take a lot longer than Charley had first thought. The im-
mediate task of cleaning out all the wreckage and hosing
the place down was hard back-breaking work, but pre-
sented few difficulties. Drying out the downstairs was the
real problem. The trouble was that the salt water had pene-

trated the stonework, and it was virtually impossible to get rid of it. Mildew appeared, and though this brushed off easily, it was not possible to paint or repaper the walls as they were so slimy. An official from the Housing Department told Charley that nothing could be done about it. They would have to build a false wall inside the rooms, that stood clear of the real walls and left a space for air to circulate between the two.

The breaches in the sea walls on Flatsea were not completely repaired until the end of March, and none of the inhabitants was allowed back permanently until then. It was an unhappy, frustrating time for the family, particularly when Pat and baby Kevin came home. David's house was just too tiny for all of them, and Doris, Charley, Aaron and Peter moved into the camp where Grandpa and Grandma were living. There were many other problems too. The amount of damage had to be worked out and claims made on the insurance; money had to be borrowed from the bank to tide the family over; and there was new furniture, carpets and curtains to buy. On one dry, frosty afternoon Peter lit a huge bonfire of paper, books, disintegrating furniture, old rags, everything that was useless but could be burned. Most heartbreaking of all to the family was the loss of some of their treasured personal possessions. The destruction of all the family photographs Doris took particularly hard, all the pictures of her wedding and her children at different stages of growing up. Charley never found his ring. He spent hours hunting for it, prising off drain covers, poking rods down pipes, even searching the mud at low tide, but it was nowhere to be found.

Even when they moved back it was a long time before things were normal, as every downstairs room required the building of second walls. Charley's plans for a party were postponed until the summer. The number of events to celebrate had increased, not only Martin's wedding and Aaron's eighteenth birthday, but Peter's sixteenth, and his own wedding anniversary.

Everything was still except for the gentle rise and fall of the swell. Susan lay in the bottom of the boat, eyes half-closed, absorbing the heat. Peter gazed intently down at the sea-bed, which shifted and rippled as the sea heaved.

'There it is again! It glinted, I'm sure. I'm going in.' He lowered himself over the side. Susan opened her eyes and stared out at the horizon where a long wrinkle on the surface and a crowd of gulls, their wings beating, indicated a shoal of fish.

Peter surfaced. 'Only a piece of tin,' he gasped.

'Let's go ashore. You've been trying for hours.'

'It must be somewhere.'

'I don't think we'll ever find it. At least your dad was able to buy another.'

'It can't ever be the same as the one Mum bought him all those years ago.'

'No. It's rotten luck. I suppose he should never have taken it off. I'd never take mine off, never.'

Peter looked at her and smiled, then pulled the boat in towards the sandhills. It ran aground with a dry, rasping sound. He jumped out and pulled it up the beach.

'The new walls look impressive.' They were higher and thicker; the sea-facing side was all concrete, right the way round the island. They stood some way inland; between them and the sea were the saltings, and mud-flats and creeks that were covered by most high tides, leaving little islands of sea-grass.

'It's a perfect summer day.'

'Dad and I sometimes fish here, when the weather's like this. Let's lie in the dunes. The sun will dry me.'

'School on Monday.'

'Not for much longer. I'm sorry we're both leaving.'

'Why?'

'We shan't see each other every day.'

'We will in the evenings. It's exciting. Both starting to earn our independence. Will you be happy?'

'Building boats? Yes. Will you be in an office? In and out of Oozedam every day?'

'I don't mind. Coming home will be good, you at the pub not fifty yards off.'

'We've known each other six months now.'

'Six months? We've known each other for years.'

'It's six months to the day the floods came. That's when it really started. I'm grateful to that tide.'

'You're the only person in England who'd say that.'

'I don't care.'

'We're different people from six months ago,' she said. 'We're growing up.'

'I can sometimes almost sense it. I suddenly realize my bones, my skin, they're a week further away from childhood. I sort of wait inside myself and watch it happening ... I want to find that ring.' He walked towards the boat. 'It's the party tomorrow, *the* party. If only I could give Dad back his ring tomorrow evening! He's grieved about it so much.'

'All right then, one more try.' She helped push the boat back into the water.

Oozedam, grey and smudgy, shimmered distantly in the heat. It looked tired and shabby and old, ready to sink again under the waves. There was not a cloud in the sky.

The blue above was immense, resting on a circle of land and sea.

'This is the life,' said Peter.

'Something foul happened at school yesterday,' said Aaron. 'Shall I tell you?'

'Of course.'

'A note in my desk. Typed, unsigned. "Only white scum reckon black trash." Not the first time either. If I knew who it was I'd turn him into pulp. And I'd rather enjoy doing so.'

'It might be a girl.'

'I'd turn *her* into pulp.'

'Just ignore it. It isn't the end of the world. It's never worth fighting about that.'

'Do you get insults like that?'

'No. People in Oozedam get on with us well enough. Maybe whoever wrote that note was jealous. Some ex-girlfriend of yours. I'm not your first girl, Ron.'

'No. I'm not your first boy either.'

'Only one that matters.'

'Listen. There's something else I must tell you. More important than that note. I leave school this month. I've decided I'm going to London.'

'London! Have you got a job? You never said.'

'No, I haven't. But I will. It would be nice to do something with music, my guitar, though I don't suppose there's much chance of that.'

'What do your parents think?'

'Give me a chance ... I haven't talked to them about it yet. But you've got to some time, leave home, I mean.'

'And me too.'

'No, no! Just wait, I haven't finished. Whether I go or

not depends on one thing. Will you come with me? You could find work there ... will you?'

'Of course I will.'

'It would be a good time to end it, if you wanted.'

'End it? No. What about you?'

'No. Definitely not. This means ... we really are serious, doesn't it?'

'Yes.'

'Well, I sold it. Twenty-five pounds.'

'Twenty-five pounds!' Ann said.

'Yes, quite handsome. Though I hate parting with it. Particularly as it's us, this room.'

'Do you remember that bookseller in Royal Street who couldn't bear to part with any of his books? The one who went bankrupt and became a librarian? Perhaps you ought to be a curator in an art gallery.'

'No chance. End of next year, I'll be painting, full-time.'

'How will we live?'

'I'll do any work I'm offered. Sign-writing, posters, anything. And there won't be any more nights away from you.'

'Are you going to charge Lynwyn for this?'

'I can't.'

Ann looked at the portrait of Aaron. 'It's the best thing you've ever done.'

'It's taken me a hell of a long time.'

'Why's it such an odd shape? I've never seen such a long, thin thing. A canvas over six feet in length, and it can't be two feet wide.'

'He's a long, thin person. Metaphorically, I mean.' He painted a few delicate strokes of pale yellow on Aaron's hair.

'I don't understand.'

'This picture's turned out to be what I feel about him, rather than a real portrait. No. Perhaps that's what a real portrait is.'

'Isn't that his voice, downstairs?'

'Yes. I'll bet he's told Dad he's staying the night with us. I wish he wouldn't do that.'

'Why?'

'Because he stays with *her*.'

'Does it matter?'

'No. But it annoys me, all the same. He uses people.'

'Lynwyn?'

'No. He loves her. I think. Odd. Even Mum's got used to the idea. Her son and a Jamaican girl. It must have alarmed her. She's funny. She can be dead against us doing certain things, then when she sees we're determined to do them, she'll champion us against all-comers.'

'That's mother-love.'

'I suppose it is.'

'Are you taking the picture to the party?'

'Yes. It's finished.'

'Six months to the day since the great tide.'

'Which was more important to us than anybody else.'

'Why?'

'It decided you to marry me. Is that hair too pale?'

'No. He's almost albino. No? Flaxen? It's about right. Yes, we got married. I think now we should have done before. I was silly. Frightened of tying myself. To you! How absurd.'

'I think you were right. We're only twenty now. We needed that time. Supposing it had all gone wrong? Much more difficult then, being married, than sharing a room.'

'There's a long time ahead for things to go wrong.'

'You don't think they will, do you?'

'No. Though nothing is for ever. We've a fair chance.'

'I think we have.' He stood back from the picture and looked at it for a long time. 'It's finished,' he said.

The party was on a Sunday night because the pub closed half an hour earlier than on weekdays; the celebrations could begin as soon as the bar was tidied up. The family had all assembled long before this, however, and were enjoying themselves in the private part of the house. Baby Kevin was the centre of attention; all the women were thoroughly spoiling him. That afternoon he had sat up for the first time: it was a marvel. Grandma left at about half past nine. It would soon be her bedtime, and she did not altogether approve of drinking late on a Sunday night. Others could do so; she had resigned herself to that a lifetime ago, but she would not. On this special occasion, though, she thought Fred could be permitted to stay for as long as he liked; if he was asleep beside her in the morning that would be good enough, this once. She wouldn't even mention the subject.

At ten o'clock all the tables were removed from the bar and stacked outside in the shed, and the chairs pushed to the side of the room. The bar was to be used for dancing, and Aaron's Rod was providing the music. The house was full of bustle and excitement. There were all the regular drinkers as well as friends of Charley and Doris and friends from school and college, people of all ages. In the kitchen every surface was covered with refreshments; Doris presided over her two daughters-in-law and Susan and Lynwyn, issuing a stream of orders and directions. This had been the pattern for the women, on and off, all day. Now everything was ready.

The bar was soon full of dancers. Those who just wanted to talk and drink stayed in the sitting-room. Charley, hurrying from one room to the other looking for Doris, almost bumped into Peter.

'You look very excited, son. Enjoying yourself?' They had to shout, the music was so deafening.

'I am. I've an announcement to make later.'

'What about?'

'A surprise.' He laughed. 'Don't look so worried.'

'I hope I shall like it.'

'I can guarantee you will.'

Doris was in the kitchen, alone, looking out of the window. 'Charley, Ron's told me about this idea. London.'

'Yes, I know.'

'Well, what do you think?'

'That if it doesn't work out he'll soon be back here. Anyway, I've told him he's not leaving home till he gets a job there first.'

'London. Vice and drugs.'

'We must learn to trust him.'

'He's very young.'

'Eighteen. That's an adult nowadays. Come and dance with me.'

'What, to this noise? I wouldn't know where to begin. Oh, all right.'

In a pause in the music Lynwyn held something out to Martin. 'It's for the picture. Ron said to give it to you. Go on, take it! He earned it last week at the club.'

'I don't want it.' He gave it back to her, but she pushed it down the top of his trousers, and hurried away. He pulled it out. Two five-pound notes.

'Peter has an announcement to make,' Aaron shouted over the talk and laughter. 'Silence for my kid brother.'

'What's it all in aid of?' Doris asked Charley.

'I dread to think.'

'On the night of the flood,' said Peter, 'a very precious object was lost in this house, and it was never found. I've been looking for it all these months, and ... er ... Susan's been helping me. We found it this afternoon. We were out in a boat, just off Dangie Point, looking down into the water. There's some shingle there on the sea-bed. Anyway, there it was, in the stones. Heaven knows how it got there, but ... Dad! Your wedding-ring.'

Charley put a hand on the counter to steady himself. Doris threw her arms round him, but he was too overcome to hear what she was saying. Everyone was applauding, shouting, laughing.

Peter was standing in front of him. 'Hold out your hand, Dad.' He did so, and Peter eased the ring onto his third finger. 'Now you're legally married. Speech!'

'Speech, speech, speech!'

'I just don't know what to say,' Charley stammered. 'Thank you. No, I just don't know what to say.'

'That's exactly what he said at our wedding,' Doris whispered to Ann.

'Say nothing, lad,' said Grandpa. 'You're behind that bar. Give everyone a drink instead. Start with a big one for Peter.' Charley obeyed.

Grandpa left at about half past midnight. He went home by an unsteady, circuitous route that took him to the sea wall; he had had more than enough to drink, and a little night air would help before he faced the music. No, she wouldn't be playing the harmonium at this hour surely; the music he could hear was Ron and his friends. It was a brilliant moonlit night, and another very high tide, just like six months ago, except that the sea was now a quiet continuous rustle. Everything was normal: telephone wires back in their places, hedges and fences repaired, lights across the water. It was a very hot night, almost too hot for walking. July heat-waves, that meant a wet August. The insurance had paid better than he'd hoped. All those costly repairs to the house; he hadn't had to pay a penny. Of course there were many precious things they weren't able to replace. Bessy had been upset about that. But the old sampler had washed and ironed out well; she had sewn up the tears and he'd reframed it himself. It was hanging now over Peter's bed. Amazing how well the harmonium had dried out. Sounded a bit wheezier, but that suited it; Bessy herself was wheezier. Peter had been pleased by that old sampler. Grand boy. His only regret was he wouldn't live long enough to see Peter's children. Martin's maybe, but not Peter's. There wouldn't be enough years. All those grandsons now married or with girls; that was a reminder how time was sliding. There'd be many more great-grandsons; Browns always had boys.

He climbed unsteadily onto the top of the wall. Good thing he'd remembered to bring his walking-stick. The tide was not far below him, but it wouldn't come over, perhaps never would again. These new walls were stouter than he could have imagined possible. But they say nothing can ever be sure of keeping out the sea if it really wants to return and claim its own. Some people said the land was tilting, but how could that be? Nature just came back at times and took its revenge, that was all.

Two people stood on the wall, away to his left, lovers, arms round one another, kissing. Careful, she might fall backwards into the sea. Who were they? Any of the young people from the party – not Ron and Lynwyn; he could still hear the music. David and Pat, Martin and Ann, Peter

and Susan? No. Yet they looked familiar. He strained his eyes. Charley and Doris! He felt embarrassed, an intruder, as if their emotions should somehow be kept more private than those of their children, and he hurried down the bank and went home.

About the author

David Rees was born in 1936, and went to King's
College School, Wimbledon, and Queens' College,
Cambridge. He taught in schools in France and London,
and is now a Lecturer at Exeter University.
Since 1975 he has published eight novels for Children
and teenagers.

His hobbies include surfing, listening to music and
tracing the family tree. Mr Rees is married and has
two sons.

Heard about the Puffin Club?

... it's a way of finding out more about Puffin books and authors, of winning prizes (in competitions), sharing jokes, a secret code, and perhaps seeing your name in print! When you join you get a copy of our magazine, *Puffin Post*, sent to you four times a year, a badge and a membership book.

For details of subscription and an application form, send a stamped addressed envelope to:

The Puffin Club Dept A
Penguin Books Limited
Bath Road
Harmondsworth
Middlesex UB7 ODA

and if you live in Australia, please write to:

The Australian Puffin Club
Penguin Books Australia Limited
P.O. Box 257
Ringwood
Victoria 3134